To Kyle

Voices On the Bay
Ginny Russell

Ginny Russell

Beach Holme Publishers
Victoria, B.C.

This edition is published by Beach Holme Publishers Ltd.
4252 Commerce Circle, Victoria, B.C. V8Z 4M2,
with the assistance of the Canada Council and the B.C. Ministry of Tourism and Culture.

Editor: Guy Chadsey
Production Editors: Elspeth Haughton
Sarah Dodd
Cover Art: Judy McLaren
Line Drawing of Reid's Roost by Anthony van Tulleken
Illustration on page 41 by Daryl Hunter

Canadian Cataloguing in Publication Data

Russell, Ginny, 1931-
       Voices on the bay

        ISBN 0-88878-343-4

    1. Indians of North America--British Columbia--
    Gulf Islands--Juvenile Fiction.
    I. Title.
    PS8565.U87V6 1993   jC813'.54   C93-091526-7
    PZ7.R87Vo 1993

For my family,
with love and thanks.

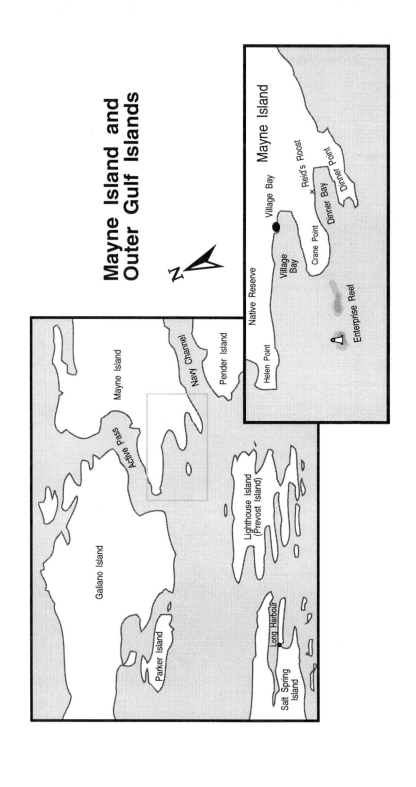

Mayne Island and Outer Gulf Islands

N

Mayne Island

Mayne Island

Village Bay

Reid's Roost

x

Dinner Bay

Dinner Point

Crane Point

Village Bay

Native Reserve

Helen Point

Enterprise Reef

Mayne Island

Navy Channel

Pender Island

Active Pass

Galiano Island

Parker Island

Lighthouse Island
(Prevost Island)

Long Harbour

Salt Spring Island

Anthony van Tulleken

One

"You'll have a great time," Dad reassured him at the airport. "Quit feeling sorry for yourself. Besides, your grandparents are expecting you."

All the way to Vancouver, Dave's stomach felt queasy. Usually he loved flying, but this time it was different. He had too much on his mind. When he came back to Toronto next week, it would be just in time to watch the stupid moving van loading their things. Why did they have to move? And to Chicago, of all places!

He knew he'd *never* find new friends like Jason, Nate and Thang, *never*....

Since the plane landed, he'd been too busy to think about anything. Right now, he had real problems. He almost fell out of the boat trying to save the flashlight.

"Sorry, Aunt Morna, it went straight to the bottom." He straightened up and grasped the motor handle again, his sopping sleeves dripping all over his jeans. "I wasn't expecting that big wave. Wow! Which way now?" he asked, squinting at the darkening shoreline.

"Straight ahead. You steer. I'll tell you where. We'll be fine, honestly."

"We will?" Dave wasn't so sure. And he certainly didn't like somebody telling him where to go. But he and Aunt Morna were alone, and the choppy waves seemed more menacing, now that the sun had gone down. That last big wave had been a surprise. Good thing they had lifejackets on. His teeth chattered and he hunched deeper inside his turtleneck sweater.

"Are those the lights from the ferry dock at Village Bay?" Anything to keep his mind off the darkness and the waves.

"Village Bay? Yes, that's where your ferry came in this afternoon."

"I didn't see any village."

"Indians used to live there, that's all I know. Ask your Gran and Grandad when we get back."

"You mean *if* we get back." He could hardly see the shore, and they must be almost on top of it. He could hear the waves sloshing against the rocks.

Should he edge over to the right? It was only a few hours since he'd arrived on Mayne Island for the first time. The shoreline and the little motor boat were both strange to him.

2

He even felt uneasy about his grandparents. This afternoon, when his plane arrived in Vancouver he realized, with a shock, that it had been a long time between visits. Gran and Grandad had been away in Australia for more than three years. They'd written letters, but that wasn't the same.

By now they were almost strangers. Gran looked just as he remembered her, her grey hair always falling out of its top knot, but he hardly recognized Grandad. His hair was getting thin and he didn't seem as tall as he used to be.

At least he knew Aunt Morna. That was another reason he didn't want to move away from Toronto. She often came there to film TV sports news. Last year she'd taken him to the race track, right up with the roof top camera. When she'd agreed to take him fishing this evening, he'd been delighted.

And the fishing had been *great!* It was only later that things went wrong. He shivered, tried to squeeze the water from his soggy sweater, and gripped the handle of the motor so tightly that his knuckles hurt.

"Keep well away from this headland on your port side," warned Morna, over the noise of the motor. "Once we're past that, just swing around into Dinner Bay. Then you can hug the shore. But not too closely."

Dave mumbled to himself, *OK, Captain, but I don't know why you can't steer this stupid boat. You're the one who knows these waters. And how about the flashlight?* Should he tell Grandad first, and then buy a new one, or the other way 'round? *It's not my lucky day.*

The engine coughed. Dave held his breath until it sputtered back to its regular rhythm. He stared at the cliffs that loomed high on his left, as he eased around into Dinner Bay. The land seemed even darker and more dangerous than the ocean. He tried to keep his voice calm.

"Are we nearly there?"

3

"Yes, almost. Hey, Dave, I said *hug* the shoreline, not *kiss* it! You're too close. Sorry I can't help. I didn't tell you before, but I cut my hand, when I was cleaning the fish. It's bleeding. I have to use my other hand to keep the pressure on it. Slow down!"

He managed to cut the speed without stalling the motor. "How much further?"

"Just keep your eyes peeled, right where the water meets the land. It's the only dock with a sailboat. You'll see the mast."

Dave was afraid to blink. He kept his eyes fixed on the murky shore. *I'm a jinx*, he told himself. *If I hadn't asked to go fishing, she wouldn't have cut her hand.*

"Hey, Aunt Morna, I can see the sailboat now, and there's the dock. And about time! I thought we were going to end up on the rocks." He put the motor in neutral gear and glided in slowly, behind the bigger boat. "Whew!"

"I *told* you we'd make it," said Morna, as Dave grabbed hold of the dock. "You're getting the hang of it. Soon you'll be handling the boat like a pro."

He felt better. It had been scary, but he'd made it. Maybe he was a jinx, but he wasn't a total pea brain. Aunt Morna gave him the feeling there was hope for him yet.

"Course I was a bit scared," he admitted, as he tied the mooring lines and bundled the fish into plastic bags. "Oh look, there's a light from the house. They should have turned it on earlier. We could have used it as a beacon. Gee, it sure is a long way up."

He cupped his hands and yelled, "Hello up there, we're back, and we caught two big ones! Salmon. Come on down and have a look."

They hurried along the floating dock, Morna still gripping her cut hand, and Dave carrying the fish. He shivered again, partly from relief, and partly because he was so wet.

4

At the bottom of the metal ramp that led to shore, he stopped in surprise. "It's a lot steeper than when we came down. The tide sure makes a difference."

"This isn't Lake Ontario, Dave. This is the Pacific Ocean! Hey, take it easy," warned his aunt. "I fell off this ramp last week."

Dave wasn't listening, and she nearly fell off again, as he dashed past her, pretending to be a tightrope walker. He was so pleased with himself. He hadn't wrecked the boat, and they had two fish.

"Yeay! We made it," he shouted, stepping onto dry land. "Aunt Morna, did you know there are a hundred steps between here and the house? I counted them on the way down."

Grandad clumped down the last few steps. "Ninety-nine, to be exact. I know, 'cause I built 'em," he said, as he rescued his glasses from the end of his nose. Then he aimed his flashlight inside the bags that Dave was opening. "Well done, you two! Who caught the whopper?"

"I did, Grandad. Course I needed a bit of help pulling him in. Nearly thirteen pounds. That's about six kilos! We weighed him already."

"And who's going to gut those gorgeous salmon?" It was Gran, calling from half way down the hill. "I love eating 'em, but I sure hate cleaning 'em, and Grandad's got a sore thumb."

"Don't worry, Mother," called Morna. "Dave looked after the boat on the way home, and I gutted them." She gave Dave a quick poke with her elbow and whispered, "don't mention the cut on my hand."

He whispered in Morna's ear, so Grandad couldn't hear. "The flashlight's a secret too. I'll buy him a new one first."

He shouted up to Gran, "We gave all the fish guts to the seagulls. Yuck! They'll eat anything! That's a great fishing spot, Grandad. Hey, Grandad, what do you know about the Indians, the ones who used to live in Village Bay?"

"Not much to know," mumbled Grandad. "Just that they're supposed to have been there. Not worth spending a lot of time investigating, I expect. And besides, if we ever get some sailing weather, we'll be too busy. We'll be at *least* three days, messing about in the San Juan Islands."

Too bad, thought Dave. He loved sailing, especially 'messing about' in new places. And he'd asked to go to the San Juans. But whenever anyone told him something wasn't worth his time, it made him stubborn.

Now he really *did* want to know more about Village Bay. But not right this minute. First things first. "Race you up to the house, Aunt Morna? Can't wait to eat my fish!"

"Goodness gracious," sputtered Gran, as he ran past her, "does that boy ever slow down?"

Two

Of course, he won the race. And he was first to open the kitchen door. Warmth from the wood stove met him in a welcoming wave. Luckily the kitchen was large, because the old-fashioned stove, nicknamed 'Monster', took up a quarter of the space. It stood high off the floor, as black as coal, and very fat.

Dave stripped off his soaking sweater and edged close to Monster, to toast his backside. Gran got busy. First she grabbed her sharpest cleaver and Dave's prize catch. Slicing through back bone and all, she cut off nine pink slices, thick ones.

"You're lucky, folks. Salmon steaks are quick cookers," she said, as she sizzled them in butter, and rescued the rest of the meal from Monster's warm belly. "Sit down and dig in."

"Too bad about your sister," Grandad said to Dave. "I know she wanted to go fishing so badly. When she phoned about the chicken pox, she was crying."

"Yeah, poor old Susie. Boy, is she spotty." He piled his mashed potatoes into a volcano. "Pass the butter please. I'll write Susie a letter, when I get time. Boy, this fish sure tastes great when you catch it yourself. Or even when you catch it with your aunt," he added hastily.

Grandad laughed. "I remember once, when your mother was about your age, Dave. She was fishing all alone, from a row boat, and she caught a whopper like yours. Well ... she stood up to show it off, and ended up...."

"Upside down. I know," said Dave, grinning. "Mom's always telling us that story."

"Bet she didn't tell you the best part," added Gran, between mouthfuls. "After your Grandad helped her to rescue the boat, and the fish, she wouldn't eat even one bite."

"She had a cheeseburger!" snorted Morna. "We teased the heck out of her."

"Mom's still not crazy about salmon; but I am," said Dave, glancing at his grandmother. Gran slid the ninth and last piece onto his plate. "Wonder if I have room for three of those butter tarts for dessert? Did you remember how I like my butter tarts ... lots of raisins and...."

"No walnuts," chanted the rest of the family.

"I marked it right beside the recipe, when you were just a little tad," said Gran. "No walnuts for Dave, but double the raisins."

"Now that we're nearly stuffed, tell us more about the fishing," said Grandad. "Lots of boats out tonight?"

"To start with, just us," said Dave. "And Aunt Morna caught the first salmon as soon as we got there."

"*And* dropped my yellow hat in the water, but good ol' Dave fished it out," said Morna.

"Then," said Dave, his voice rising and his arms

waving, "I spent *half an hour* landing the big one. After that, it got *really* crowded. Boats from everywhere, like a five o'clock traffic jam, straight to our spot. One boat bumped into us, and our lines got all tangled."

"Then while I was gutting the fish, a ferry came along," said Morna, "and couldn't get through the narrows, because of all the fishing boats."

"So the captain sounded his horn, five blasts. Aunt Morna says that means 'You're standing into danger'. In other words: get out of my way, right now!"

"Speaking of ferries, here comes mine," said Morna, peering through the front window. "Gotta dash. Our news crew's covering canoe races, starting tomorrow. I'll come back on the weekend."

"Thanks for taking me fishing, Aunt Morna." When he gave her a hug, he noticed that her hand was bandaged neatly. The old folks hadn't even noticed.

"When you come back, Aunt Morna, I'll tell you what I've found out about those people who used to live in Village Bay."

She chucked him under the chin. "Forget it, Dave. You'll probably find something better to do. Anyway, I don't know how you'd go about it. Finding out, I mean." She grabbed the plastic bag, with her salmon inside, and dashed for the door.

"*Now*, we can relax," said Gran. "Just plunk yourself down by the living room fire."

Dave added another log first, and watched as the dry alder wood snapped and crackled in the grey stone fireplace. The reddish light cast shifting shadows on the walls and ceiling. Gran pulled her armless rocking chair close to the fire, and spread her knitting across her lap.

"I'm so glad your parents said you could come by yourself, Dave. Even if it *is* for less than a week. Goodness sakes, dear, you look like you're ready for bed. It's been a busy day."

9

Dave tried to look wide awake, but it was an effort. His eyelids felt heavy.

"Unusually cold tonight," said Grandad, throwing more wood on the fire. "But tomorrow, we're due for summer weather again. If there's enough wind, we might get off on our sailing trip. San Juan Islands, here we come."

That's what we planned, thought Dave. *We've talked about it on the phone for months.* But now he had a feeling that he'd rather stay right here.

Mayne Island was so *different*, and he'd hardly had time to explore it. Especially that bay they called Village Bay, and *especially* when everyone said it would be hard to find out about it. But Grandad's feelings would be hurt if he asked *not* to go sailing. Dave sat down beside his grandfather on the lumpy old sofa.

Oh well, whatever happened, there was nothing he could do about it. Everything in his life seemed to be out of his control, these days.

"That old sofa's a terrible eyesore," said Gran, with a sigh. "We should give it away."

"Not on your sweet life!" said Grandad, sternly. "It's perfect. Purple and green are my favourite colours. Matches my old plaid shirt. And besides, if we had a new one, nobody'd be allowed to eat on it, or snooze on it with their shoes on." He nodded firmly to Dave.

Dave smiled. He was beginning to feel a little more comfortable with his grandfather. It seemed they both liked things to stay the same. Too much change was hard on a body. Maybe they could work things out, so there'd be time for everything, sailing *and* investigating.

He sank back, and the cushions sagged with him. Gathering his courage, he said in a low voice, "I really meant it, Grandad, when I said I was interested in the Indians who lived around Village Bay." Grandad seemed to wake up a little, and Dave continued.

"A few weeks ago, I was reading this story about a cabin boy who was supposed to be on Captain Cook's ship, when he met the Nootka Indians. It was really interesting. You said there wasn't much to know about the Indians that lived around here. Don't you know *anything?*"

Grandad took a minute or two to poke the fire. He seemed to be collecting his thoughts. Dave looked at his grandmother. There were two things he remembered best about Gran, from his younger days. One was her springy grey curls that were always trying to break loose from the knot she twisted on the top of her head.

The second thing he remembered was that Gran *usually* had something to say about everything, even without stopping to think.

He wasn't at all surprised when she said, "Of course, dear, Village Bay would be a perfect spot. It's near the narrows where the salmon always pass. And there are cod and other fish around here too, and clams, mussels, crab ... and there used to be lots of oysters as well."

"Middens, that's what they left behind," muttered Grandad into his newspaper. "Know what a midden is Dave?"

"Mitten? Did you say mitten?"

"No," said Grandad, smiling, "M-i-d-d-e-n. You'll find 'em all around these islands, not just on this one. They're sort of garbage dumps, actually ... just piles of shells left over, after the insides got eaten."

"The Indians only needed a few of the shells for containers and tools," added Gran. "So they had lots left over. Not far from Village Bay, you'll see a sign for the Helen Point Reserve. It means that land's reserved for Indians. We'll have to find out if any of them still live there."

Dave was only half listening. He was watching Gran's knitting. He knew she was making the sweater for him.

He wasn't quite sure if he was going to like it. It was awfully bright. Not at all like his favourite old blue one.

She had six different colours of wool, and each colour was wound around a plastic holder. The holders swung back and forth as she rocked and clicked her needles. It made him ... sleepy ... watching the colours jiggle.

He said, "I 'member, once, in a museum, I saw ... some Indian ... tools...."

Gran looked at him over the top of her glasses. Dave seemed to be asleep, sprawled sideways across the arm of the sofa. His eyes just wouldn't stay open, and the cushions were soft.

"Don't wake him, dear," Dave heard Gran say softly. "Just sort of ... unbend him, and take off his shoes. He's had a busy day. I reckon he's been up for at least eighteen hours, if you add in the time change between Toronto and here."

She tucked a blanket over him. Then she pushed his fair hair back from his face. "I'd never dare to do that, if he was awake," she said, fondly. "He smells a bit fishy, doesn't he? But I guess he'll keep 'til morning."

"That boy's still a perpetual motion machine," said his grandfather, proudly. "Remember how bouncy he was before we left for Australia? That was more than three years ago. I was afraid he might be growing out of it. Remember on the ferry ride from Vancouver? He talked a lot, but he sat so still. Too bad he's upset about moving to Chicago."

"But after he got to the island," Gran whispered, "I could see that he still had the same old energy."

"Did you see how much *wood* he chopped, after he had his swim?" Grandad sounded amazed.

"Yes dear, I couldn't believe it! He's still your kind of boy. You'd think he'd take it a bit easy, the first day. Four hours on the plane, and then the ferry ride. Of course he had to go swimming. I can understand that. But wood chopping and fishing too?"

12

Dave was almost asleep, but he could still hear. He kept his eyes shut, and breathed deeply, in ... and out. The sagging sofa felt like a feather bed.

Grandad closed the fire screen and turned off the lights. Only the dancing firelight lit the room. He spoke in a whisper. "Yes, that boy's full of the old bounce."

Dave couldn't catch what Grandad said next. Something about the plans for tomorrow.

"We'll tell him at breakfast," said Gran.

Tell me what? he wondered. But his grandparents had disappeared and he was asleep before he could even guess. He was only vaguely aware of the phone ringing, just before daylight. *He* thought it was part of a dream.

Three

It was the sun, streaming full in his face, that finally woke him. *So that's why I was dreaming about forest fires,* thought Dave as he threw off the covers. *Oh, oh! The sun will melt those chocolates Mom sent.*

He rescued them from his bulging back pack and stuffed the sticky box into the refrigerator. Then he rummaged in his pack again, for some clean clothes. Even he could tell that the ones he'd slept in were fishy. Then he slid open the glass doors, and tiptoed out onto the verandah. The dew felt cool on his feet.

Below him, Dinner Bay was a sheet of glass. On the far shore, every tree and rock had its double. Nothing moved. Not a needle stirred on the cedar tree that towered beside the house. He knew they wouldn't go sailing today.

That was good, wasn't it? Now he'd have time to find out something about Village Bay.

He heard scratching noises, somewhere below him on the hillside. A squirrel? Or maybe a deer? He'd really like to get close to a deer.

With his elbows on the railing, all he could see below was a tangle of trees and bushes, no animals of any kind, no ninety-nine steps, no slippery sloping ramp. If he leaned a-w-a-y out, he could just see the end of the dock.

Last night he'd moored the motor boat there, in the dark. How had he ever managed to do it?

That reminded him that today he'd buy Grandad a new flashlight. Come to think of it, why couldn't he see the stern of the motor boat? He was sure he'd tied it right at the end of the dock. Now it was gone.

Maybe his knot wasn't the right kind, and it had come....

"Can't you smell the bacon?" Gran was calling. "Breakfast's ready."

"Just a sec. Something I have to do first," he shouted back. The missing motor boat forgotten, he dashed to the fridge for the chocolates, and then to his back pack, for two more presents. He put a large photograph beside Gran, a small glass bottle beside Grandad, and the chocolates exactly in the middle.

At last he plopped himself down, and plunged straight into his bacon and eggs.

"Doesn't this child ever take it easy?" Gran asked Grandad. "Your mother was such a slow-poke, Dave. Oh look! Susie sent me a picture of her class. 'The last day of school', she's written on the back. That's why the kids are smiling. Too bad she's not here."

"Next year for sure," said Dave, suddenly feeling guilty about his sister. She was nearly five years younger, only nine. At first he liked the idea of being the only one to come to Mayne Island, but already he missed her, a little. She always encouraged him when he had crazy ideas.

"You can't get chickenpox twice, can you, Gran? Wait'll I tell Susie about this place. She'll never believe those rocks! That cottage you rented one summer, on Okanagan Lake, it wasn't like this at all. Had a sandy beach, and no rocks and no tides!"

"That was ... four years ago, before we went to Australia," said Grandad. "Hope you like this place too."

"Maybe even better. We'll see," said Dave. "Next year, I'll take Susie fishing, eh, Grandad?" He smiled, thinking of a few good ways to scare her.

"Sure," agreed Grandad, "you're a salt water fisherman now. Hey, Dave, thanks for bringing this bottle of Real Ontario Maple Syrup. Pancakes for breakfast tomorrow. And chocolates too? Thanks Dave."

"Sorry they got sort of ... squished. Dad sat on my pack, at the airport. Mom forgot to tell him about the chocolates. Then they got sort of ... melted a bit. Say, I thought I heard a deer in the woods. After breakfast, I'm...."

"After you've checked for the deer," Gran interrupted, "perhaps you'd like to go over to Salt Spring Island with your grandfather."

Dave remembered the motor boat with a sinking feeling. They'd need it for the trip. What had happened to it? There was too much going on, here on quiet old Mayne Island. He couldn't keep track, from one disaster to the next.

Sure, he could afford a new flashlight. But a new motor boat? That was out of the question. But it was no good playing innocent. He'd have to own up.

"You look positively ill, Dave," said Gran, peering at him. "Maybe you'd better stay here. Grandad has to take the ferry over to Salt Spring to buy a new shackle for the sailboat. We can't use the motor boat. One of the neighbours borrowed it early this morning, because his needs fixing. Did the telephone wake you?"

He explained that he thought it was part of his dream. But what was really great was that the motor boat hadn't drifted away, after all. What a relief. And now he'd get a chance to buy a flashlight, while Grandad was buying his sailboat shackle.

"Problem is," said Grandad, sounding upset, "I've just discovered the rudder needs repair work too. I'd waste most of the day, going to fetch the shackle. I really ought to stay here."

Grandad looked at Gran appealingly. *She* looked as if she'd rather not go either.

"Why don't I go by myself," volunteered Dave. "Just tell me how to get there and what to buy."

Grandad looked relieved, found a map, and suggested that Dave take his rusty old bike, because it was quite a few kilometres across Salt Spring Island, from the ferry dock to the town.

Dave checked the tires, and oiled some of the worst squeaks. The handlebars seemed a little wobbly, but he thought he could manage. He still had ten minutes to look for the deer, before he had to leave.

After a quick search, he found the place that Gran had recommended, a twisted Arbutus tree, gigantic and so bent over that part of the trunk lay flat on the ground. You could crouch down behind it, and be out of sight. Usually that spot was downwind of the forest path, so the deer couldn't smell you.

Safely hidden, all he saw at first was a mother raccoon, trailing three, no ... four, babies. They scrambled up the hill to the tallest cedar tree. Near the top, they seemed to have a resting place. He didn't see them come down again.

Maybe the mother was Grandad's favourite, the one he had named Miranda, because she'd chosen to live under the verandah.

But where were the elusive deer? He'd have to be quiet, if he really wanted to see them. Dave hardly ever stayed still, or stopped talking long enough to listen for anything. Next time, perhaps, he'd bring a book. Do two quiet things at once.

He craned his neck to look out over Dinner Bay, catching sight of a crested diving bird, blue, with white markings. He was sure it was a Kingfisher, the same as the ones he'd seen often in Ontario.

He could recognize its loud chatter, even with his eyes closed. One of his favourites, a real go-getter. Dave watched while the bird hovered, dove, and came up with a herring in its beak.

"Good catch," he whispered to the Kingfisher, "but I'd rather have salmon! Oh, oh. Someone's ringing the brass bell on the verandah. Guess it's time for me to go."

"Lone explorer sets off for the unknown," remarked Gran at the top of the hill, as she handed him his jacket, the map and a lunch. He chuckled to himself. When he was little, Gran had always made simple things seem more daring. She was still at it.

He gave her a big grin, waved goodbye and pedalled off down the dusty road. He met no one, just two chipmunks and a squirrel, on his ride to the dock.

The ferry was ready to leave, so he only had time to peer at the Village Bay beach as he hurried on board. *The village that isn't there*, he mused. Maybe before the ferry dock was built, he might have seen some signs of a midden.

Why do I even care? he asked himself. *What's so fascinating about this old bay, anyway? I'm just pretending there's some kind of mystery here. Grandad's probably right. Not much to know.*

He went to the top deck and leaned out over the rail. Now he could see the swirls in the water, as the Captain backed out, turned around, and headed the *Queen of Nanaimo* out of Village Bay.

He couldn't believe this was the same water that had seemed so scary in the dark. Of course it was windy last night, and the choppy waves had almost swamped the little motor boat. Today, the sea looked as smooth as melted butter, if butter could ever be greenish blue. Even the high cliffs, some rocky, some forested, looked safe.

"Sorry," said Dave, as he almost tripped over another boy who had leaned over to tie his shoe. The boy straightened up to his full height, at least a half a head taller than Dave.

"It's OK, it's a free country," said the taller boy, half grinning.

"I've never been to the Gulf Islands before," said Dave, as if that explained everything. "Sure is a neat part of the world, eh?"

"I don't think you're American," said his companion, eyeing Dave carefully. "Bet you're from the mysterious East. Eastern Canada, that is."

Dave wondered how anyone could tell. Did he have *made in Ontario* on his forehead?

"Yep, I'm from Toronto. But I've been in Vancouver quite a few times. My grandparents used to live there." Why did this big kid have to be so nosy? "You ever been east? Want to see a big city? Get a load of Toronto! Vancouver's not half the size." The boy looked unimpressed.

"In Toronto, we've got everything," Dave said proudly. "Our stadium's called the Skydome, because it's got a retractable roof!"

"Who *cares*. I like to play baseball in the real outdoors. This place is for me. I was born right here on Mayne Island. Rick's my name, if you want to know." Rick put down his heavy pack.

"Lots of neat things around here," declared Rick. "See that beacon away out in the channel? That marks the far end of Enterprise Reef. And see that green buoy, floating at anchor, closer to us? That marks *this* end of the reef. Otherwise you'd never know the rocks were there."

"Yeah, it's what you can't see that's dangerous," said Dave, shuddering. He was quiet, watching the waves the ship made as it plowed its way across the busy channel. Already three more ferries were in sight.

His grandfather had told him, jokingly, that the British Columbia Ferries had a bigger fleet than the whole Canadian Navy. He'd have to check on that when he got a chance.

But not from Rick. He probably wouldn't know important things like that. "So, you live here?" he said to Rick. "They got a school on the island?"

"Just up to the ninth grade. I go to Salt Spring Secondary. Next week, I start grade eleven."

"I'm just starting grade nine," Dave confided. "Will you go on this ferry every day?" he asked, thinking how much fun that would be. And it would be a lot warmer than Dave's long trudge to school in the snowy Ontario winter.

And who knows *how* far he'd have to walk to school in Chicago? There it was freezing *and windy too.*

"Actually, us school kids have a special water taxi," said Rick. "It's called the Scholar Ship. Good name, eh? Should be about half a dozen of us from Mayne Island this year."

"Hey, neat! Do they ever have to cancel the taxi? Like, in bad weather? I wouldn't mind missing the odd day of school. Unless it was in the baseball season."

"Once in a while we can't go. If we have storm force winds; or if the roads get too icy for the ol' school bus to get us down to the water taxi," admitted Rick. "It freezes around here once in a while. Some winters we get a lot of snow."

Rick looked at Dave intently and said, "Hey, if you're from Toronto, you're a Blue Jay fan, right? Me, I like baseball too. I pitched a no hitter last year." The tall boy pushed his sleeves up and went through the motions of his best pitch, right there on the slanting deck.

"Catcher's my favourite," said Dave, stretching to catch an imaginary pitch to home plate. "Too bad we can't play. Say, Rick, I don't suppose you know any Indians? I got interested when I heard about the village. You know, Village Bay?"

"There's no village there now," Rick said gruffly. "What sort of stuff you want to know about Indians? I might be able to...."

"Oh you know," interrupted Dave. "Like, what kind of life did they have? Pretty primitive, I'll bet. No electricity, not much of anything, 'cept totem poles and smoky wooden houses. I've seen pictures of Indians around here wearing capes made of cedar. Must have been pretty itchy."

Rick turned to face Dave, and looked him straight in the eye. "Why do you want to know about the Indians, anyway?"

"Just got curious when I heard they used to have a village in the bay."

"Must have been a long time ago," Rick said dreamily. "Lately they've lived on the Helen Point Indian Reserve, over there." He was pointing to the green shore to the right of Village Bay. It was just off that shore where Dave and Morna had caught their two salmon last night.

"How many Indians live there now?" asked Dave.

"Not sure, exactly. Not many that live there all year round. Indians don't have to live on the Reserve, you know. Anyhow, I'm not the best person to ask, because I've never bothered to find out much."

"Oh, well," Dave sighed, "too bad." He'd been hoping there were hundreds of Indians over there, and maybe he'd see some of them launching their canoes, or....

Probably Grandad was right, he was thinking. There were better things to do with his time. "I suppose before the white people came, their lives were pretty miserable," Dave suggested.

"Miserable?" Suddenly Rick appeared agitated. He put his hand on Dave's shoulder and seemed to be peering inside his brain. "Listen kid," he said finally, "I think you've already made up your mind about Indians. I don't think you'd listen if...."

"I would, I would," protested Dave. "I *like* investigating things." Last Christmas holidays he'd taken a toaster and an alarm clock apart, and got them back together again, much to his mother's amazement. But Rick was shaking his head.

"I think you're just a nosy kid," Rick said at last. He sounded disgusted. "Not worth my time trying to explain, even if I could."

Rick looked more sad than angry as he shouldered his back pack and strode off without warning. All that Dave could see of him was his huge pack, with RLJ stencilled on the flap.

Dave called after him, "I only wanted to ... to...."

"Forget it," Rick mumbled without turning his head. "Ask someone else." After he'd disappeared, Dave felt more confused, the more he thought about it. Rick had seemed like such a great kid at first. Really, he hadn't meant to be rude.

All he'd said was.... What *had* he said? He couldn't remember, exactly. Something about the Indians having no electricity, or being pretty primitive.

Maybe it was just that Rick didn't want to be bothered with strangers who invaded his special island. Or maybe Dave had been bragging too much, about how great

Toronto was. Was that it?

Oh, nuts, bumbling Dave is at it again. I'm really good at putting my foot in my mouth, and I don't even know which foot I put. He felt awful.

Thank goodness he hadn't told Rick his name. Or had he? Maybe they'd never meet again.

"ATTENTION PASSENGERS," boomed the loud speaker. "WE ARE NOW ARRIVING AT LONG HARBOUR, ON SALT SPRING ISLAND."

Dave joined the throng of hikers and bikers waiting to go ashore. *One flashlight, and one stainless steel shackle. Should be able to get those without getting into trouble.*

Four

He knew from his map that it was a long ride to town, at least half an hour, on Grandad's wreck of a bike. That was fine. It was a perfect summer day. There was no deadline, except the four o'clock ferry back to Mayne Island. He had new roads to explore, even side trips off the main road.

He took time to climb a rocky hillside, following a disappearing deer. He inspected a few old boats, abandoned along the shore. On a deserted beach, he collected shells and sat down to eat the lunch that Gran had packed. This was the life.

Last week in the sweltering Toronto heat, he'd been earning summer money washing the neighbours' windows, and helping his Mom, grudgingly, to pack china in boxes. Next week he'd be helping to load the car for the long drive to Chicago, and saying goodbye to everything that was important. What *was* the name of that girl that smiled at him at Jason's house last week? Susanne, or Sue Anne? Hmmmm.

Right here on this quiet shore, it didn't really matter. This was another world entirely. Not part of the past, not part of the future.

He sprawled on the sand. Airplane jet lag, three hours worth, was still with him, even if he didn't realize it. Sleep came easily.

"Ten after three!" he discovered when he woke up. "Better hurry." He pedalled back to the main road and headed for town. In the hardware store, he found the right shackle for the sailboat, but no flashlight. All sold out and no time to look for another store.

He'd ridden half way back to the ferry dock, when, with no warning, the handlebars on the old bike fell off with a clatter. He looked everywhere for the bolt that had fallen out, but it was nowhere to be seen. Better to push on, he decided. No time to go back to a bicycle store in town. It was awkward, pushing a bike with its handlebars off.

As he trudged along, he passed an old man who was fixing a gate. Dave gave a friendly wave, and the old man called out, "Hello, young fellow. Got a problem, I see."

"Yes sir. Lost a bolt."

"Well now, sonny, why don't I look in my grandson's tool shed?" Before Dave had time to protest, the old man had ducked into the shed and lugged out a heavy box full of bicycle parts. "Anything there that would do, sonny?"

Dave hated being called *sonny*, but a new bolt would be great. "Thanks," he said, "I'll take a look. Hope I don't miss the ferry. It's twenty minutes to four."

"No, it's not. It's twenty minutes to three."

"No kidding? Yesterday, on the plane, I must have set my watch wrong. And just now, I fell asleep, and I thought I'd been asleep for hours. What do you know about that!"

"So, you've got loads of time. Here's the right size bolt, I think. Now fix your bike quick, and come and have a glass of lemonade." The old man straightened up and headed to the front porch.

Dave followed, and while they sat and sipped, Dave explained where he was from, and why he was visiting Salt Spring Island.

"Me too, I'm just visiting," said the old man. "Helping my grandson fix his house. My home's over on Vancouver Island. Now there's a big island! Two hundred and eighty miles from top to bottom."

"Yeah, I remember in this book I was reading about Captain Cook. Didn't he go up the outer coast of Vancouver Island and meet the Indians at Nootka Sound? Around ... 1778, somewhere around there." Dave didn't say, but the things he'd read in that book were almost the *only* things he knew about the history of British Columbia.

"Ha! Captain Cook, great discoverer," scoffed the old man. "Well, I guess he was a great traveller; went all over the world. But think about it the other way round. 1778 was when the First Nations People discovered *him*! Cook and his men didn't even get the Indians' name right," he scolded.

"Those British sailors stuck the name Nootka on them, and their real name is Nuu,Chah,Nulth. They've got their proper name back, you'll be glad to know." His crinkled face got more lively as he talked. Now he seemed to be enjoying Dave's startled expression.

Dave swallowed and cleared his throat. *Could it be?* he thought desperately. This was important, and he didn't want to say the wrong thing. After his ... ummm ... misunderstanding with Rick, he was wary.

The man seemed friendly enough, but would he like it if Dave asked questions? Maybe he was the sort of person who liked to do all the talking.

"Did you want to know if I'm a Nuu,Chah,Nulth Indian? Well, the answer is no. I'm one hundred percent Indian, all right, but I'm one of the Saanich People. Some white people call *all* of us around these parts the Coast Salish People. They think we're all alike, but we're not. To me, it's the Saanich part of the Coast Salish that's important. Name's Bill Allen."

"Dave Jones." They shook hands formally. Mr. Allen was the thinnest person Dave had even seen. His hand was like a bundle of dry twigs, but surprisingly strong ones. Dave couldn't believe his luck. Here was an actual person from one of the First Nations, a real Indian.

He looked older than Grandad, but his mind seemed to be just as sharp. He had more hair, too, salt and pepper, and spiky. One of the Saanich People, eh? Maybe *he'd* have some answers, if Dave could just ask the questions without goofing.

Dave cleared his throat and was about to speak, when Mr. Allen suddenly slipped away into the house.

When he came back he was carrying a small wooden canoe, about a foot long. "My great-great-grandson made this," he said, smiling broadly, "only eight years old!" Dave was impressed. It was beautifully made.

"From cedar wood?"

"Red cedar. Like our big canoes. Yellow cedar's better for the paddles, though." Dave felt the smoothness of the soft wood. Had Mr. Allen said his great-great-grandson made it? How old would that make Mr. Allen?

"I'm ninety-five," announced Mr. Allen, guessing Dave's thoughts. "I'm allowed to brag," he added. "And I can still pitch a mean baseball. The Raccoons made me their honorary coach. They're the junior team, over on Vancouver Island."

Dave's mind was still on canoes, skimming over the ocean waters. "Were the old time Saanich canoes anything like the ones the Nootka made?" he managed to ask. "No, sorry, I mean the Nuu ... Nuu,Chah,Nulth. And does anybody still make those big ones?"

"Actually there's lots of different First Nations along this coast. They each have their own languages and customs, like the special shape and design for their canoes. Ours are quite plain, just a cedar dugout, with a long low pointed prow. We didn't need such big ones as the Indians that travelled in rougher waters."

Dave was remembering now. Last year their class had gone to the museum, and Nate and Jason had sketched a Haida canoe, and he and Thang had chosen a Kwakiutl one. Some people spelled it Kwagiutl. He'd forgotten that he knew those names.

He wondered if Mr. Allen had a small canoe of his own, when he was a boy. Had he helped to make it? Had he fished for salmon? So many questions, but he was afraid to ask.

"When we were kids," Mr. Allen was saying, as he poured Dave some more lemonade, "my pals and I went crab fishing in the winter in our canoes. We'd put a big empty oil drum in the bow of our boat, and keep a fire going inside it." Gave heat and light." He paused to blow his nose.

"For firewood," he continued, "we had to gather roots from the Douglas fir trees, roots that were full of that sticky pitch. They burned the best. I can still taste those crabs my mother cooked. Mmmmmm." He closed his eyes and licked his lips.

Dave closed his eyes too. He could see Mr. Allen, just a boy, racing up a distant pebbly beach, bringing his mother the crabs. He could even imagine his mother's face, smiling her thanks.

"It was worth the cold canoe trip, "continued Mr. Allen. "We still make big canoes, you know. We have races every summer, all up and down the coast."

Dave was glad that the old ways weren't being forgotten. He glanced up at Mr. Allen's weathered face and risked a question. "Don't suppose you know anything about the Indians who used to live at Village Bay, over on Mayne Island? I guess they were from a different group." He was hoping Mr. Allen might have met some of them in his travels.

Mr. Allen seemed to be having trouble with his smile. Or perhaps he wasn't feeling well. After all, ninety-five was pretty old. Maybe he should be having a nap? Dave watched anxiously while Mr. Allen rocked his chair back and forth, his eyes fixed on some far away point. He rocked for ages without saying anything.

"Maybe I'd better go now," Dave said quietly.

"No, no, don't go yet. You've still got lots of time. I'm remembering things I thought I'd forgotten. Things from my childhood, about my parents, and my family." His voice cracked.

"Where was I?" Mr. Allen asked Dave. "Oh yes, two of my aunts died of smallpox before I was born. We didn't have any immunity to white people's diseases, you see. Later on, we all got vaccinated. Ouch!" he said, clutching his upper arm.

"But sonny," he continued, fixing Dave with a piercing glance, "the important thing for you is that I was born there and I lived there off and on, until I was twelve."

"There? Where?"

"Right there, not far from Village Bay. The Saanich People have fished there since time began, well almost. The Cowichan People too. My mother was from a Cowichan family. They're part of the Coast Salish group too, and close neighbours. Sometimes we worked together, especially in the salmon netting season. We lived at the Helen Point Reserve, but I heard stories about an old village, down near the ferry dock."

Dave beamed. *So there really was a village there once, if*

29

he's right. "Tell me about the fishing," he urged.

"Well, my Dad and the other men would go out in their big canoes and stretch their drift nets across the narrows. Needed lots of strong men and lots of canoes. Hard work in those currents, but we sure caught a lot of fish. Later on, our drift net fishing was banned by the gov'ment, but I can remember, as if it was yesterday. Mayne Island was Lotus land to me. Some of the white people still call it that."

"You mean, like, it had everything you needed? Fresh water, loads of trees and animals and fish and berries, stuff like that?"

"Yeah, stuff like that, 'specially the salmon," said Mr. Allen, licking his lips. That started Dave dreaming again, a fisherman's dream. He could hear the shouts of the men in Mr. Allen's father's boat, as they neared the shore with their catch.

He could picture a young Indian boy and his brothers. He *had* to have brothers. Dave could picture them standing on the beach, wishing they were old enough to catch the fish.

"Pay attention, Dave," said Mr. Allen quietly. "I'll tell you about my name in the Saanich language. It means 'coho', that's a kind of salmon."

"And there's sockeye and chinook too," added Dave. "Chinook's what my aunt and I caught last night. Chinook have black gums and coho have white."

"Well, I was named after the coho. THAA,WEN, that's my name, in the Saanich language," he said, getting up and tracing it in the gravel beside the porch. "It has a double meaning, because it also means the south end of Mayne Island, which is where I used to help unload the fishing canoes."

"Weren't you old enough to fish with the men?" Dave asked.

"Went three times, that summer I turned twelve. Hard work, but I was ready for it. It was great. Now about my name, Dave. Names are very important to us. Always spell mine with capital letters, do you hear? That's the way we do it. And the comma shows that you have to take a quick stop in the middle."

T-H-A-A, comma, W-E-N. Dave traced it and repeated it softly. "THAA,WEN." The first part, the THAA, sounded like the first three letters in ... 'theft' and the WEN sounded like 'when'. Maybe that would help him remember how to say it. "Suits you better than Mr. Allen," Dave said.

"Well then, sonny, you can call me THAA,WEN, if you like. Oh, oh. It's nearly time to go. Baseball game in town. I'm sorry, we'll have to say goodbye." Stiffly, he got up from his rocker and reached for his hat, a faded blue baseball cap.

"This old cap's from when I was home run king of the Old Timers' League," he said proudly. He twirled it around on one finger and planted it firmly on his head. "There, I'm ready."

"Wish I'd had time to hear more about the old days, when you were a boy," said Dave as they walked out to the road. "Like what games you played on Mayne Island."

"Sorry, kid. Say, we *could* get together day after tomorrow, if you like. I'm going over to Mayne to see my old buddy, Nick Dominic. Blue house high on a hill, near the church. How about coming over there after lunch?"

"Will if I can." Dave nodded eagerly.

"Meantime," added Mr. Allen, "I suggest you spend an hour sitting on the Village Bay beach. Early morning's the best. My pals and I, we had this great game we played all over the island, and it was all because of that very bay, the way it's shaped."

"Eh?"

"Yes," replied Mr. Allen shaking his head and looking worried. "Yes sir, the shape was a real problem. But here's another clue about our game, Davey boy. Maybe this one's more helpful. Think about Killer whales first, and see where that leads you. Sit on the beach and pretend it's before any white people came."

"I will, but...."

"Oh, and Davey, the next time I see you, I'll tell you my sad story about my favourite scraper. I lost it. That all happened on Mayne Island too. Oh here comes my ride. I've got to go. 'Bye." He was in the car and away before Dave had a chance to yell more than, "Thank you!"

Scraper, wondered Dave, *What's a scraper? What did you scrape with it? Or did it get scraped?*

Maybe the old man had never really been sitting here, talking practically non-stop, not letting Dave ask all the questions he'd been dying to ask. He must have been here, if his name was still scratched in the gravel beside the porch. Dave ran back for another look.

Sure enough, there it was. THAA,WEN. And Grandad's bike sported a shiny new nut and bolt for its handlebars. No, it wasn't a dream. Before he got back on the bike, he leaned over and traced the name again, including the comma. He didn't want to forget it, or anything Mr. Allen had told him. He'd have a lot to tell Gran and Grandad, that's for sure.

Too bad the weatherman had said it would be windy tomorrow. They'd be off sailing, and he wouldn't see his new friend again. Probably he'd never find out about THAA,WEN's favourite game, or the mysterious lost scraper.

Still, Dave couldn't get over his luck. He'd actually met a real Indian, and a fascinating one at that. Now he'd better make a dash for the ferry, and just in time, too. He was the last one aboard.

On the homeward journey there was still no wind. He crossed his fingers that the weatherman was wrong about good sailing weather for tomorrow. But if it were windy, at least he could get up *really* early, before it was time to leave.

He'd spend an hour sitting on the Village Bay beach, thinking about Mr. Allen's game. At least he could give it a try. *Killer whale? What kind of a clue was that? And what did the shape of the bay have to do with anything?*

Five

Dave didn't stop talking all through dinner. First, about meeting Rick on the ferry, and their misunderstanding. Then about the handlebars falling off, and finally about Mr. Allen, his Indian name, and most of the things he'd told Dave about his life, including the puzzle about his childhood game. Somehow the game was connected with Village Bay.

Gran and Grandad looked dazed, he noticed at last. Maybe he was talking too fast? He never *did* get around to mentioning the scraper, whatever that was.

It seemed like a good idea to give the old folks a rest. So, after dinner, he ambled down to the dock, and sat in the cockpit of the red sailboat. *It really will be fun*, he told himself. *The San Juan Islands are in the United States, Washington State. I'll be living in Illinois, soon.* Crossing the

border in a sailboat would be quite different than crossing in a car.

He hopped ashore again and started off along the
forested edge of Dinner Bay. Gran had told him that the
deer followed this same faint trail that meandered through
some huge cedars and Douglas firs. It was cool and
almost dark there, and the tree tops disappeared above
him in a hazy green umbrella.

*Some of these trees are so old, they'd have been tall when
Mr. Allen was a kid. He and his friends might have chased each
other through this same part of the forest, and yelled to each
other across this very bay.* Dave yodelled at an eagle on the
far shore. Just as he'd hoped, his echo came back from the
rocky cliffs.

Thinking about shadowy Indian figures flitting in
and out of the trees made Dave shiver, not with fear, but
with a sudden feeling of disappointment. Was *that* all
there was to the game the Indian boys had played? Hide
and seek in the forest?

He climbed the ninety-nine steps once more, and
kept himself busy chopping wood, for at least half an
hour. At home he never had to think what to do with his
spare time. Often he and his friend Thang would do odd
jobs at Thang's parents' Vietnamese restaurant. Or one of
the guys, or even his sister Susie, was always around,
ready for some kind of action.

But *next week*, at school in Chicago, it would be
different. Awful, in fact. He wouldn't know anybody in
his class. And would American girls laugh at his Canadian accent? But there was nothing he could do about it
now, he decided as he put away the axe. Should he start
a jigsaw puzzle?

Instead, he found an old guitar of Aunt Morna's. He
knew only two tunes, and was soon tired of them. He'd
ask Aunt Morna to teach him another, when she came
back. Maybe 'When the Saints Go Marching In'.

Next, he took the huge book Grandad had found for him, one that might have something in it about the coastal Indians. Deliberately, he chose a hard chair, and turned it so he couldn't see Gran knitting.

Last night it was just as if he'd been hypnotized, those silly little balls of coloured wool ... jiggling. He tried to read. Maybe there would be something about Indian scrapers. If there was, *he* couldn't find it.

Soon, even the *click* of Gran's needles made him sleepy.

"Take your book up to bed, dear," said Gran, who had been eyeing him over the top of her glasses. "Still a bit jet lagged?"

"Yeah," agreed Dave, yawning. "The clock says nine, but my body says midnight!" Picking up his fallen book, he headed upstairs, after they'd agreed on a starting time for the sailing trip. Yes, it would be fine, his grandparents said, if he got up earlier and explored Village Bay, as Mr. Allen had suggested.

In bed, he read only a few pages, and before he fell asleep, he set the alarm clock for five a.m. There must be more to THAA,WEN's game, not just a chase through the forest. After all, there were the two clues. It was worth at least one early morning start.

When the alarm buzzed, he threw on some clothes and pedalled the old bike over to the only public spot on Village Bay, a flat place for launching small boats. The bay before him was deserted, except for some noisy seagulls and dozens of empty boats that bobbed up and down at their mooring buoys.

Along the shore to his right, was the ferry dock, black and massive. Dave stared at it. Maybe before it was built, there might have been something to show where a village had been.

Mr. Allen had said that when he was a boy, there was no village on the bay itself. They'd lived in the shelter of the forest, at the Helen Point Indian Reserve on the far side of the bay. But earlier, such a village must have been here, or very close by.

The gravel that scrunched under Dave's feet, black gravel, with white specks, *could* be the remains of an ancient midden. The white specks could certainly be shells, ground fine over the centuries. Clam or oyster shells, perhaps?

If this was a midden, it wasn't all *that* exciting. Dave kicked the crunchy stones. *Oh well,* he decided, *I might as well do what I came for. I'll sit here and concentrate on the old man's game.* He wiggled his back against a dry log and sniffed the salt air. *Those two clues are like signposts.*

First, the Killer whales. How could he tie Killer whales to this beach?

Maybe the Saanich People cornered them around here. Dave knew that whales came through these channels, every once in a while. He'd seen a few fins in the distance, on the way over from Vancouver. But where did the shape of the bay fit in? It wasn't shaped like a whale.

Grandad's book had suggested that the Indians on the Gulf Islands weren't big whale hunters, like some of the people from further north. Both the Saanich People and their Cowichan neighbours had other food that was more dependable, and easier to catch, right here in these sheltered bays.

Idly, he watched the waves curl up the deserted beach. Was the Killer whale just a symbol for those other Indians, the northern ones? The ones who made those big totem poles? He sniffed the air.

If this were a long time ago, before the white people came, there wouldn't be that smell of tar. That came from the timbers of the ferry dock. But he'd smell the cooking fires in the Indian camp. Especially the salmon smoking. He closed his eyes.

Salmon smoking. A sudden picture of a fat sockeye, or chinook, or coho, puffing on his corncob pipe, flashed into his mind.

He was still chuckling when he noticed a canoe slipping around Crane Point, not far to his left. The paddler was alone, and seemed to be unloading some sort of trap and attaching a white floating marker to the end of its rope.

Crab trap, that's what it is. Reminds me, I haven't caught any yet. Mom said she and Aunt Morna and Aunt Mary Jo used to catch 'em around these islands. Bet they never did it in winter, like Mr. Allen.

That boy in the canoe looked like Rick. *Hey, maybe it is him!* Dave was just getting up the courage to call out, when the lone paddler disappeared, back around the high headland of Crane Point.

Oh, well, Dave decided, *Mayne Island's not very big. I'll run into him again, sooner or later. Maybe later is better. I still haven't figured out what I said wrong, the first time.*

He was scuffing along the beach, picking up stones with unusual markings, when suddenly, with no warning, something hit him on the back of the neck. "Ouch! Well, what do you know? A seagull dropping clam shells."

He watched as two more seagulls did the same. *Oh, now I get it. They're letting them smash open on the rocks. Free lunch.* He added some empty clam shells to the stones in his pocket. *Hey, that reminds me, I haven't had breakfast! Better hurry. If the water's too choppy when we're sailing, I might not feel like lunch.*

Grandad was making blueberry pancakes when he got home. It was still only six-thirty by the kitchen clock. "Guess what," declared Dave, as he slathered on the maple syrup, "maybe Mr. Allen meant that the whale was a symbol for others, like the Haida, or Kwagiutl, or Nuu,Chah,Nulth." Gran nodded encouragement.

"And didn't some of those guys hunt whales on the open ocean, with really big canoes, and harpoons? We saw a movie about it at school." He stopped talking long enough to devour six pancakes.

"And I read in your book, Grandad, that some of them had really neat legends about whales, even if they didn't hunt them. Like, when you saw a whale it meant you were going to drown, and stuff like that. It's true. I read it in the book!"

Gran suggested, quite firmly, that one can't always believe what one finds in books. But she did agree that the idea of the whale being a symbol had possibilities. "Maybe that's the first step in solving your puzzle, dear. By the way, your Grandad and I talked it over, and we've decided...."

"We should wait 'til next summer, when Susie's here, for the big sailing trip," said Grandad, with a slow grin. "Hope that's OK with you, young fella. The San Juan Islands should still be there, unless there's a major earthquake. And somehow, I think there's lots to do around here."

Dave could have hugged him, but he wasn't sure if Grandad would like that. "Thanks, that's perfect," he said happily, as he helped himself to the last three pancakes. "Next summer will be perfect. But we can go for a short sail, can't we?"

"Any time," said Grandad.

"I was poking around that boat yesterday," admitted Dave, "and I was getting curiouser and curiouser. That name, 'Sitting Duck' sounds sort of familiar. And I haven't been crabbing yet, either. Mom says to watch out, when you take them out of the traps."

As Dave left the breakfast table he said, "You're right Grandad, there's lots to do around here. And I keep having this funny feeling about THAA,WEN. You remember? That's Mr. Allen's Indian name. I feel like THAA,WEN's right here, telling me things."

Suddenly he remembered the best part about staying home. He could talk to the old man again tomorrow, when he came to Mayne Island to see his friend. Great! He could ask some more questions. But could he figure out about the mystery game *before* they met?

He went in search of Grandad's book again, and was just settling down with it, when Gran mentioned his sister, Susie.

"Susie!" groaned Dave. He hated writing letters, but he'd promised. "Let's get it over with," he announced gloomily, and grabbed a single sheet of Gran's typing paper, and a ball point pen. "She's always complaining she can't read my messy writing, so I'll print it in big capital letters. I'll s-p-r-e-a-d it out so it'll use up the whole page."

DEAR SUSIE,

THIS PLACE IS CALLED 'REID'S ROOST', AND IT'S ON DINNER BAY. IT'S GREAT, IF YOU HAPPEN TO LIKE STEEP HILLSIDES, THICK FORESTS, CHOPPY CHILLY SALT WATER AND JAGGED SHORELINES!

HAVE YOU EVER HEARD THAT A PICTURE IS WORTH A THOUSAND WORDS?

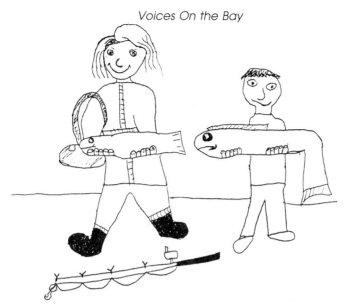

THAT'S AUNT MORNA AND ME. WE
EACH CAUGHT ONE SALMON, MINE WAS
BIGGER, THIRTEEN POUNDS (SIX KILOS)!

WHEN AUNT MORNA WAS LANDING
HERS, THAT'S WHEN HER HAT FELL IN. I
RESCUED IT, BUT IT SHRUNK ... SO SHE
GAVE IT TO ME.

YELLOW LOOKS A BIT FUNNY ON ME,
SO I'M GIVING IT TO YOU FOR A
PRESENT. IT SAYS 'HAWAII' ON ONE SIDE
AND 'SOME KID' ON THE OTHER.
HONEST, YOU'LL LOVE IT!

I HAVE TO BUY GRANDAD A NEW FLASHLIGHT. HIS IS ON THE BOTTOM OF THE OCEAN. IT WAS WIERD WATCHING THE LIGHT GO DOWN AND DOWN, UNTIL IT DISAPPEARED. AND DON'T THINK I DID IT ON PURPOSE!

YESTERDAY I HAD LOTS OF ADVENTURES. FIRST I MET ....

"Come on, Dave, you can finish that later," called Gran. "The wind's just right for a quick sail to Lighthouse Island. Meet you down beside the *Sitting Duck.*"

Six

Sitting Duck? Down on the dock, Dave inspected the red sailboat, with its thin white racing stripes along each side, not at all like a duck. "Now I know why she's familiar," he informed his grandparents at last. "She's sort of like that sailboat you got when Mom was about my age." Gran was nodding her head.

Dave was remembering a picture they had at home, of Mom sailing single handed. "I'm sure that was *Sitting Duck*," said Dave, puzzled. "This boat couldn't be *that* old. Anyway, Mom said it was made of wood, and this one's fibreglass."

"Different boat," said Grandad. "But this is the same size, and fat across the middle, like the old one."

Gran said, "The wooden one was a tired old brown boat named 'Windy', when we bought her second hand.

Your Mom insisted she looked like some kind of duck, and renamed her."

"Did my Mom always get her own way?"

"Once in a while," said Gran. "Besides, we all liked the idea. Then your grandfather painted her red, to make her feel livelier. And your mother painted the white stripes on her sides, and the name on her stern."

Dave found that surprising. Aunt Morna and Aunt Mary Jo, who were both younger than his mother, were always complaining that *she* had avoided all the chores, especially the messy ones.

Gran laughed. "Your mother thought the white stripes would turn her into a racer. And Morna and Mary Jo did a dandy job polishing all her brass fittings. And I made blue curtains for the cabin. I saved them when we sold her. See, there they are."

Dave poked his head inside the small cabin, and admired the faded curtains, the stove, icebox, sink, toilet, and the four sleeping bunks. Just right for next summer's trip with Susie.

"Time we were off," growled the Captain. "Tie that dinghy on behind, Dave."

"Dinghy? Oh you mean the little rowboat. I guess we'll need it if we go ashore."

"Might come in handy, one way or another," said Grandad. "Now, take your time, and have a good look, if you're going to help me sail her." Dave inspected the boat closely. It seemed a little bigger than the one his parents had rented for two weeks last summer, but everything seemed to work the same way.

He brushed his hand along the wooden tiller, remembering the vibrations that you could feel through a tiller when a sailboat is underway. Like a heartbeat. "Gee, Gran, this tiller's as smooth as silk."

"Should be," said Gran, "I sanded it within an inch of its life!"

Grandad shook his head sadly. "I still can't metrify your grandmother. She means a centimetre!"

Dave inspected the most important parts of the sailboat: the sails, and the various ropes that pull the sails up and down, or control their action. Grandad asked him to hoist the mainsail.

Dave hauled on its rope, until the head of the crackling sail reached the top of the mast. The west wind was coming directly over the bow, and the hoisted sail flapped uselessly.

"OK, fella, you've had time to look at things," said Grandad. "We haven't got a motor. What would *you* do, to get this ship underway?"

He'd already decided about that, thank goodness. "We'll have to tack, to the left, ummm, the port side, Grandad. Can't go to the right, because the dock's in the way. So ... we need to get *Sitting Duck's* bow away from the dock, and keep her stern end in close. Can I use this paddle to push against the dock?"

"Yes, you push off, Dave. Gran can hold the stern in. I'll take the tiller. Now the wind's getting behind the sail. Now, Dave, pull in on the mainsheet, and...."

"That's a sailor's word, sheet, Dave," Gran interrupted. "On a sailboat, it's the...."

"I *know*, Gran. It's the rope that lets the sail in and out, controls the action of the wind. And the halyard's the rope that hauls the sail up and down. Dad says names are very important on a sailboat. You can't just say hand me that thinga-majig."

As soon as he spoke, Dave was sorry. Gran was only trying to be helpful. She didn't know he knew. It was a bad habit, not stopping to think.

"Pull in the *mainsheet*, Dave, *now!*" called Grandad, sharply. "And fasten the end around that cleat. Good!"

Sitting Duck responded. She began to edge out against the waves that were small, but getting choppy. The wind was pushing from the right side of the sail, and had forced the heavy boom, and the sail, across to the left.

"Now she's awake," said Gran, grinning. *Sitting Duck* was heeling over, and all three sat on the high side to make the boat more balanced.

"Time for Gran to raise the jib," called Grandad. She hoisted up the second sail, the one in front of the mast. It billowed out on the same side as the mainsail, the port side. With two sails set, *Sitting Duck* moved even faster.

Grandad let Dave take the tiller and he gripped the smooth wooden shaft. Sure enough, there was the rhythm of *Sitting Duck's* heartbeat. He wiggled the tiller to see how the boat responded. It took all his strength to keep her going in a straight line. Just like last summer on Lake Ontario, with Susie.

So far, sailing in the ocean wasn't so different from sailing in a lake. Port and starboard were just the same, and he could feel the familiar kiss of the wind as it touched his right cheek. There was nothing like it.

"Fall off a bit," called Grandad, who had been craning his neck to watch the fluttering jib.

"What did you say?" asked Dave. He'd been day-dreaming.

"Fall off," Grandad repeated. "That means steer a little bit further away from the true wind direction. There, that's perfect. See, now the sails have lost their wrinkles. Feel the boat pick up speed? She's heeling over more too. We're getting more mileage this way."

"You mean kilometerage, don't you dear?" asked Gran, with a mischievous smile.

"No ma'am, I mean, she's going faster," said the Captain, giving Gran a wink.

Dave was only half listening, as usual. He was picturing his mother painting the racing stripes and the name on the first *Sitting Duck*. He asked Gran why they didn't call the new boat *Sitting Duck II*.

"We thought about that," Gran whispered, "but we finally decided, that this *Duck* didn't want to be second to anyone! I think of her more like a ... reincarnation."

Grandad interrupted, and told Dave that they'd be changing to a port tack soon, otherwise they'd be half way to Japan. "You keep the tiller, Dave. I'll look after the mainsheets, and Gran can look after the jib sheets. Duck your head when the boom goes across. OK, crew? Ready to go about?"

Gran took hold of the rope that was holding the jib sail securely. Dave gripped the tiller, and chose a new point to steer for, a high peak on the hills of Galiano Island, on the far side of the main shipping channel. They each called out, "Ready!"

"About go!" ordered the Captain, releasing the main sheet.

Dave pushed the tiller toward the wind, and kept on pushing it, until the boat was heading as far to the *right* of the true wind direction as it had been to the left.

Meanwhile, Gran had released the jib sheet on the port side, leaving the jib sail free to flap noisily, as the wind blew it across the bow of the boat.

At the same time, the wind, now coming across the bow from the port side, instead of the starboard, had pushed against the mainsail and its heavy boom, so that the boom came who-o-oshing across, over their bent heads.

Now Gran pulled hard on the starboard jib sheet, until she had the jib set in its new position. She secured the sheet, while Grandad secured the sheet of the mainsail.

Meanwhile, Dave kept a steady hand on the tiller. Now *Sitting Duck* was heeling over to the right. All three crew members moved over to the *new* high side, the port side, this time.

"Crazy thing, sailing," sighed Gran sinking down on

the cockpit cushions. "One minute: chaos and confusion, and the next minute, when the new course is set right: perfect peace."

They were moving fast on the new tack, with the wind touching their left cheeks. Dave headed for a green buoy anchored in the water, until Grandad warned him to fall off a bit, or they'd run straight into Enterprise Reef.

Rick, thought Dave suddenly. Seeing the buoy that marked one end of the reef reminded him of the boy who had pointed out that same hazard while they were hanging over the ferry's handrail. Was that only yesterday morning? So much had happened since then.

And it was probably right around these rocks that Mr. Allen and his pals went crab fishing in the winter, in their canoe with the fire in a metal drum.

Yes, he couldn't see it yet, but Village Bay must be just around the steep headland of Crane Point. Early this morning, when he'd been sitting on the beach, he'd been staring at this same spot from the other side. Was it really Rick he'd seen, laying his crab trap? In Dave's mind, Rick and the old man kept getting mixed up.

"In a couple of minutes," called Grandad, "we'll change back to a starboard tack and head over there to Lighthouse Island."

"It says Prevost Island, here," said Dave, peering at the marine chart, puzzled.

"Your Aunt Mary Jo renamed it long ago," Gran recalled. "We used to anchor in its bays, in the first Sitting Duck."

"How did the Indians know where all the hazards were?" Dave wondered aloud, keeping a wary eye on the markers for Enterprise Reef. "They didn't have beacons and buoys and fancy charts."

"Good question," said Gran.

Dave suspected that she didn't know how the Indians managed to navigate so well. *She must be getting old,* he thought. *She doesn't dream up answers so often.* It was sad, in a way.

Dave said, "So, when Mr. Allen and his pals went crab fishing, they'd have to keep their eyes peeled, wouldn't they? But in a canoe they wouldn't be as likely to run aground as us, in the *Sitting Duck*. No keel on a canoe. That explains why the boy I saw this morning could set his crab trap so close to the reef."

"Great place, too," said Grandad. "Local knowledge, that's what they call it. That's what your crabbing fellow had. Now you take your Aunt Morna, she's picked up lots of local knowledge. Bet you she could find our dock without a light, even on a moonless night."

Oh no! groaned Dave to himself. *Is he saying that because he knows I lost the light?* Just then, he caught sight of a white floating marker, and wondered if it was the same one the boy had put out this morning. If so, it had got loose, and was drifting out of the bay, caught by the current.

He looked at the rowboat bobbing along behind them, and had an idea. After a hurried conversation with Grandad, he pulled the small dinghy in close, and hopped in.

The current was surprisingly strong. He hardly had to row at all, on the way out to fetch the marker. It was coming *back*, with the marker in the boat, against the current, *that* was the struggle. He kept splashing himself, and the water seemed colder than ever.

And these currents were tidal. It wasn't just the wind. That's what made it different from good old Lake Ontario.

He was glad he was wearing a lifejacket. All those water safety lessons Mom and Dad had made him take were coming back to haunt him. Would this be his chance to cling to an overturned dinghy? The ocean was definitely not a place for fooling around.

At last he managed to reach the spot where the red crab trap lay just below the surface. After three tries, and a lot of circling around, he managed to grab the top ring on the trap and retie the white marker.

Rocks, lying in wait just under the dinghy, made him feel colder than ever. He couldn't believe those rocks; they were so menacing. Lucky the dinghy was flat bottomed.

"Hurry up," called Grandad. "I didn't bother to anchor, and your Gran's getting dizzy going around in circles!" Dave was halfway back to the sailboat, when he remembered he'd forgotten to read the letters on the marker.

"Now what's that child doing?" Gran's voice echoed across the choppy waves, as Dave rowed back to the marker one more time.

"RLJ. That's what it says," Dave shouted as he neared the sailboat at last. "That's Rick, that boy I told you about. The one who got so mad at me for being nosy."

Too bad that Rick wouldn't know who'd done him a favour, he thought, as he tied the dinghy to the stern of the sailboat and flopped aboard.

Now they could change tack, and head straight for the island with the lighthouse. Instead of going ashore, they decided to eat their picnic at anchor, in a sheltered spot.

Gran made him laugh, pointing out the very place where his mother had tipped her rowboat and lost her salmon.

Grandad pointed to the rocky cove where Morna and Mary Jo had put a hole in the old wooden sailboat. The Reid family didn't have a house here then, just lived aboard the boat or camped on beaches for a short summer holiday. There were plenty of family legends about their adventures.

Aunt Mary Jo's favourite remark about the Lighthouse Bay disaster was "Dave, you'd never *believe* those rocks!" Well, now he could tell her he'd seen her rocks and a few others, and he was a true believer. They looked scary all right.

Suddenly he felt chilly. Without warning, the wind had changed direction and seemed much stronger. Luckily, there were spare sweaters in the cabin.

"Weigh anchor, there's a good kid," called Grandad. "Now's your chance to sail with the lee rail under!"

Seven

So far, ocean sailing had been fun, and Dave had managed to avoid doing anything too stupid. But the homeward journey was a challenge. The wind from the new direction was strong enough to make the boat heel over at an alarming angle.

Dave couldn't *believe* they wouldn't capsize. Foamy water creamed over the low side with almost every wave. Whenever Grandad called "About go!" as they changed from one tack to the other, it took every ounce of Dave's strength to handle the mainsheet.

Dave began to suspect that Grandad *could* have kept the Sitting Duck in a more upright position. He *could* have slackened off the mainsheet. Or, he *might* have taken a reef or two in the sails, to make them smaller. Anything to make the sails catch less wind.

I think he's doing it just for the heck of it, decided Dave. *Thinks he'll give me a scare.*

"Sure is fun, Grandad!" he yelled. "Susie would have a fit, if she were here. She can shriek like a banshee. Boy, I hope we can do this next summer!"

"Sure takes your mind off your other worries," laughed Gran, as the white waves piled in. "This boat's a British design, made for the gales of the North Sea, so she's quite safe with the lee rail under." Gran was soaked from head to toe, but seemed to be enjoying it.

"Look," she called, "this last tack will bring us right home. Who's that, pulling up his crab traps near our dock?"

"Mr. Sharp," said Grandad. "Hey, Dave, maybe he knows something about the Indians. He's lived here for centuries. See there's his house, next to the old log cabin. You should talk to him."

"I'm still trying to figure out exactly what game Mr. Allen played. Maybe I'll talk to Mr. Sharp later. Right now I want to check out this sailing chart. Might give me a clue. OK if I take it up to the house?"

But first, he had to help Grandad take down the sails, and bring the sailboat safely into the dock. *Tomorrow, I'll buy that flashlight,* he told himself again, as they slipped smoothly past the motor boat's empty space. *Maybe there's a store right here on this island.*

Wringing the water out of his sweater and squelching noisily in his soaking sneakers, he dashed up the swaying ramp and on up the hill, with the chart under his arm. Miranda, Grandad's favourite raccoon, scampered off the verandah railing as he came near.

He started to spread the charts on the picnic table, but something distracted him, something that buzzed past his ear, and then disappeared again.

"Hey, Gran, I'm being dive bombed," he shouted down the hill, as it happened again. "Was that a humming bird? I could hardly see. He only has two speeds: hover and *zzzzzzzzzzzzoom.* Hey, your hummingbird feeder's empty. Want me to fill 'er up?"

"No thanks, dear," puffed Gran, as she struggled up the hill. "Some people say you shouldn't feed them this late in the summer. Encourages them to stay around, instead of going south. Other people say it doesn't make any difference. I'm not sure which is right."

"Wow! His wings flapped so fast I could hardly see them. Is that what makes the humming sound? The wings?" No answer. Gran had disappeared.

He slouched down into Grandad's old canvas chair, forgetting the charts, and began thinking about Village Bay again....

The ancient settlement, before white people were around to disturb the scene ... the Saanich People and the Cowichan People gathering their supplies for the winter: salmon, berries, special plants that were good to eat ... their worries about raids from their neighbours....

In his mind, he could see a line of six or seven large dugout canoes approaching stealthily and bursting on the village from the left, around the high headland of Crane Point. Disaster!

His thoughts were interrupted again. This time the shadow of flapping wings fell across his lap, and a Bald eagle settled at the top of the same tall cedar that the raccoons liked to climb.

Wish I were an eagle. From away up high, with my eagle eye, I'd be able to see everything. Even what's behind that old log cabin at the end of Dinner Bay. He smoothed out the chart, and found the spot.

If the cabin wasn't there, I'd be able to see across that low spot, all the way to the channel between this island and the next one. Then I could tell if any boats were coming. He closed his eyes.

Before him passed, *not* the sailboats and power boats and ferries of today, but those very dugout canoes he'd just been picturing. *Suppose they really did paddle along there?* He checked the chart. Navy Channel, that's what it was called, and the island across the channel was Pender Island.

Yeah, he breathed, getting more and more excited. *Sure! Suppose they came up Navy Channel, between Pender and Mayne? Then they'd slip around into Dinner Bay, right down there, in front of me. They'd probably wait there for the slowpokes to catch up, or until it was just the right time.*

Dave could picture them vividly. They'd wait for daybreak. Then they'd make their surprise attack, sweeping around Crane Point, right into Village Bay. *That's* probably what Mr. Allen meant about the shape of the bay being a problem. When you're in it, you can't see what's coming from your left, before it's too late. Yes! He'd figured it all out, or had he?

He took the chart indoors and found the letter he'd started to Susie. On the back of the letter he made a rough sketch, copying the curves of the bays from the marine chart. As he worked, his ideas became clearer. One thought lead to another. He ran back outside and jumped up on the picnic table, where he sat as still as a stone statue. His newest idea gave him goose bumps.

So ... the Village Bay guys know their camp's in a dangerous spot, so naturally, they'd have lookouts. That's obvious, even to a pea brain like me. So ... why not put one of the lookouts over here, somewhere on this hill? When strangers came up Navy Channel, the lookout could race back and warn the camp. Wow!

Dave could see the lookout, probably a young boy. *Wouldn't it be neat if it was one of Mr. Allen's ancestors. This is before his time, of course.* Dave felt a tingle at the back of his neck. It was as if an unseen someone was here, behind him, encouraging each new idea.

Dave's mind clicked forward, from long ago, up to the time of Mr. Allen's childhood. Maybe the deer weren't the only ones that made these trails in the woods. Maybe

THAA,WEN and his friends played right here, on this hill? *They'd have heard lots of scary stories about those earlier raiders,* thought Dave. *He and his friends could have made it into a game. I would. And what do you bet that the best part of his game was being the early warning lookout. Yeah!*

It could have been right here, where the house stood now. Dave was sure that even if nobody had *told* Mr. Allen that this was a good place, he'd choose it himself. Why? For the same reason his ancestors did, because you could see straight through to Navy Channel.

"Bingo," shouted Dave. In his excitement, he knocked the letter and chart off the table. He scrambled to pick them up. "I know I'm right," he shouted to the wind. "It's logical!" That was one of his Dad's favourite words. He did research too.

But his Dad was always double checking, wasn't he? Even things that seemed logical had to be verified. Maybe he should make sure about the raiding business.

He found the book he'd been reading earlier, and spent twenty minutes digging through it. At last he found what he'd hoped to find.

"Aha! I was right, at least if this book is right. Just because it's printed, doesn't mean it's true. But this book says, 'raiding to steal and to take slaves, was once a common practice between different groups all along this coast.' "

Hurray! Probably all the school kids in British Columbia know that. But I can't help it if I'm from the mysterious East!

He dashed off to find his grandparents. In a great rush, he told them what the book said about raiding being a common practice, and his own idea that Village Bay would be easy to attack from around Crane Point.

For a little while longer, he'd decided, he'd keep his theory about the Dinner Bay lookouts and Mr. Allen's lookout game just to himself. It was his own personal discovery. It certainly wasn't in any book. Anyway, someone else might laugh. It was only a wild guess.

Right now, it seemed like a good time to relax and think about something else. Upstairs, he thought he'd seen some kids' books, real story books.

Yes, he was right. In the bookcase beside his bed, he found one of his old favourites, *The Case of the Careless Carpet Beetle.* Inside in large scrawly letters, it said:

PROPERTY OF LINDA REID

ANYONE STEALING THIS BOOK WILL BE

CURSED FOR LIFE!

And there were six ugly beetles, drawn with black crayon, marching across the page. *So, Mom liked this one too. But wait'll I tell her I saw her scribbles and her beetles! She's always telling us not to mark in books.* "Ha!" he chortled.

He'd take the book down to the deer watching place at the bottom of the hill. His brain could do with some 'down' time. And besides, it would prove to Gran that he wasn't always in a hurry.

After all, he was on Mayne Island time, and everybody knows that's not like *real* time. Tomorrow would be soon enough to worry about the flashlight and finish his letter.

And the best thing about tomorrow was that he'd see Mr. Allen again. Then he could test his idea, his own solution to the clues the old man had suggested. He started to tiptoe down the zigzag steps, v..e..r..y slowly ... just to show that he knew how ... in case anyone was watching.

Eight

He was only half way down the hill, when Gran called, "Yoo-hoo, Dave! Surprise!"

"Rats," he muttered. He'd hoped for a little more time to himself. He clumped back up, just in time to see a boy in a black cap squealing his bike to a stop, beside the kitchen door.

"Richard and Dave, I'd like you two to meet," Gran said cheerily. "Your last names are both Jones, but that's not the reason. Richard told me once that his grand-mother was one of the Saanich People. Maybe, he can answer some of your questions, Dave."

Richard, looking suddenly startled, dropped his bike with a clatter and pulled off the cap that had shielded his face.

Thud. Dave dropped his book on his bare foot. His toe

hurt, but not as much as his stomach. It felt as if it was full of lead. *Oh no. It's him, Rick, the boy from the ferry!*

Now Dave understood why Rick had been angry. But how was Dave supposed to know his grandmother was an Indian? *Now* what should he say?

Richard shuffled his feet and looked as if he would rather leave than stay. He said absolutely nothing.

Gran looked completely confused. *She* said nothing, and Dave's mouth was so dry, *he* couldn't even smile. Finally, he nodded hello, as he watched the older boy warily.

Rick's tanned face turned a shade darker, and he spoke at last, in a low voice. "So, it's you! *Dave, eh?* You never did tell me your name. *Dave!*" The way he said it made it sound like a swear word. Rick kicked his bike and looked more and more unhappy.

Who feels worse, Rick or me? wondered Dave. *Is he going to pick a fight?* Rick would win. There had to be a way to patch things up. Maybe if they could start all over again, pretend they'd never met before.

"Hi, um Richard," Dave managed to croak, "um ... glad to meet you. Say, did you go crab fishing today? Thought I saw you, about five-thirty this morning, setting your trap in Village Bay."

"Matter of fact," said Rick, still looking fierce, "a funny thing happened. When I went back for my crabs an hour ago, I had two beauties, but I could tell that someone had been tampering with my marker."

How the dickens, how could he tell? Dave wondered. His hands were sweaty and his knees felt weak. *What if Rick finds out it was me? He's not skinny like me, and he's got real muscles.* Dave prayed that Gran or Grandad wouldn't say *who* had done the tampering. Dave looked at them, panic stricken, pleading with his eyes.

"Matter of fact," Grandad began. Dave froze.

Now I'm in for it! he thought.

"Matter of fact," Gran continued breezily, "when we were out sailing, we saw your marker floating loose. And believe it or not, Richard, one of our crew rowed over, and tied it up again."

Rick looked at all three of them. He seemed puzzled and confused, but finally his face crinkled into a crooked smile. "Is that a fact? Your crew member needs a lesson in knot tying, if neatness counts. But at least it was better than my knot. Must have done mine in a hurry, since it came undone."

"Could happen to anyone," said Dave, feeling much more like his old self. The knots in his stomach were starting to unwind. It looked as if Rick was willing to be polite, if not friendly. That was a start. Rick seemed to be relaxing, now. He'd settled down on the verandah steps, and now he was taking the apple that Gran offered.

Dave wasn't home free yet. Rick probably still thought he was rude and nosy, because of the way he'd been talking about the Indians. So, his grandmother was a Saanich Indian! Naturally, he'd take Dave's questions personally. It would be good if they could find a way to really talk.

"OK with you folks, if I take Richard, umm, Rick, down to the dock?" asked Dave. "We've got a few things to sort out."

"I'll get you a snack," said Gran. "Growing boys need energy. It's a nice change for you to have another boy around, Dave." She bustled inside and came back with cheese and crackers and more apples, and the two boys tramped down the steps.

Deer watching will have to wait, thought Dave. *This is too good a chance to miss. Now how the heck can I ask questions without sounding nosy? Hmmm. If I can just get Rick started ... who knows? Maybe he'll be like Mr. Allen, full of interesting stuff.* But first to patch up their bad start.

"Sorry I flew off the handle, on the ferry," said Rick, before Dave had a chance to speak. "Don't get me wrong,

Dave, I don't really mind people being curious about Indians. The real problem is, I'm starting to realize I don't know much."

Rick tried to loosen his collar. He seemed upset. "I'm three quarters white," he explained, "and for most of my life I wasn't even interested in who Granny was. We all loved her, and the only thing she was famous for was being the one you could always count on for a hug. I wish I'd known her better."

Rick looked sad, and Dave didn't know what to say. Wisely, or not, he said nothing.

"Anyway, kid," Rick continued. "Tell me what you've been doing, besides skulking around rescuing crab trap markers? What did you do on Salt Spring Island, that day you were on the ferry?"

Here goes, thought Dave, nervously. *Now I'll know what he really thinks!*

"Have some more cheese?" he asked first, stalling while he decided how much to tell. "What did I do on Salt Spring Island? Well, it was like this:" He told Rick all the ordinary things he'd done, and then started on the special part, about his handlebars coming off, and then meeting the old man, because of it.

"You'd never believe he was ninety-five, Rick! He's as sharp as a tack. And he told me he was born on Mayne Island, right near Village Bay!"

"What's so great about that?" said Rick, lying flat on the dock, with his hat over his eyes, still devouring the last of the apples. "Lots of people were born here around that time. Grandad says at least a hundred people had come by the turn of the century. Some came as early as the 1860s. Farmers, fishermen and loggers like my great-

great-grandad. There was a post office, a school, even a jail, before 1900."

"A jail?" Dave was impressed. That was more interesting than a school.

"And right up the hill from Village Bay," continued Rick, "there was even a boarding house for tourists, for heaven's sake. They came over from Vancouver on paddle wheel steamers. It wasn't exactly the middle of the wilderness."

"Rick, listen, I'm not talking about new settlers, I'm talking about the people who were here before the settlers, and were still here when the settlers came. The man I met is one of the Saanich People, like your grandmother."

"Don't tell me," said Rick, sitting up suddenly, "have to hand it to you, Dave! You're going to investigate the Indians whether we like it or not."

Dave started to apologize, but Rick stopped him. "It's all right, kid, don't get your shirt in a knot. I think I understand. For you, this is all new. Probably very few Indians in your tidy little part of Toronto."

Dave had to admit that he didn't know of any. His pal Thang was Vietnamese, and he knew lots of kids from lots of different countries. But Indians? The only ones he'd seen were downtown at the bus terminal.

"Anyway," Rick said, sounding impatient. "What did the old guy tell you?"

"What didn't he? Mr. Allen was a great talker. He...."

"Allen. That wouldn't be Bill Allen? Tall, and soooo skinny you can practically see through him? Spiky hair? Usually wears a baseball cap?"

"Yeah, that's the guy! Sounds like you know him."

"I'll tell the world! When I was four years old he scared the heck out of me, showing me a gigantic stone axe. You won't believe me, Dave, but he's my grandmother's uncle! Ninety-five? I thought he'd be a hundred and five by this time. He's a great spinner of tales, is Bill Allen!"

"Wow! This is incredible, Rick!"

It took Dave ages to tell Rick everything that Mr. Allen had told him, especially the puzzle part, about the old man's childhood game. "He made me curious, even more curious than usual, giving me those clues about Killer whales and the shape of the bay!"

Rick gave a muffled "hmmmm." By now he'd finished all the food and was lying flat on his stomach. Dave couldn't tell for sure whether he was really listening.

Very patiently, in logical steps, Dave tried to explain how he'd started to think about the shape of Village Bay, how it was dangerous because you couldn't see your enemies coming until it was too late.

"Yeah," agreed Rick, sounding at least alive. "Crane Point is so high and so close to the beach, they'd be there before you knew what hit you."

"Mind you," said Dave, trying to be fair, "I'm not saying who the enemies were. Just some other group who were famous for being whale hunters, or ones who had whales in their legends, maybe. This part of the story goes 'way back, before the Indians around here had settlers to worry about."

He had to admit to Rick that the book he'd been reading was a bit fuzzy about raiders. "Let's just say they could have been from *one* of the other First Nations, or different ones at different times," Dave said cautiously.

"Sharing the blame?" Rick suggested.

"Sort of," confessed Dave. He wished Rick would sit up and look more interested. It was hard to talk to someone who seemed half asleep.

"Yeah," Rick agreed, between yawns, "sharing the blame sounds like a good idea. It's ancient history now. Anyway, away back then, the Indians from the Gulf Islands weren't blameless either. They raided other people, so I've been told. That's the way life was in those days. But tell me more about the game. Did you solve the puzzle?"

"You *could* say I'm still guessing. But what if Mr. Allen and his friends used those stories about enemy raiders? I bet they heard lots about the old days from their parents and grandparents!"

"Like, around the camp fires, eh?" mumbled Rick.

"Sure, why not," said Dave, defending his idea. "The older people passing on their history by telling stories. The kids would love stories about raiders. They'd make up games. Some of the kids could be the raiders, and sweep around Crane Point and attack the camp. And some of them could be lookouts, saving the camp. Eh? What do you think, Rick?"

Dave sucked in his breath and waited. He hoped Rick didn't think he was a complete loony.

Rick yawned again, a gigantic yawn. After a moment he said, "Yeah, kid, I like your story. It may not be the right answer, but it's possible. My friends and I, we played that kind of game when we were younger. Now we're too old for fooling around. Are you going to ask the old guy if you're right?"

"Tomorrow. He's coming to visit a man called Nick Dominic. He said to come over after lunch, if I liked. But there's more. Listen, this is the best part."

Dave seemed to have caught Rick's attention. Instead of sprawling along the dock, the older boy sat up, wide awake.

"Well, let's hear it then!" Rick demanded.

Dave continued, in a whisper. "A perfect place for a lookout would be away over here, in Dinner Bay, because you could see the raiders' canoes as they slipped by that low part, at the end of the bay. Before white people built that log cabin, it would have been easy to see Navy Channel from the top of the hill."

"Hold on, Mr. Detective. First question," Rick barked. "Why would the raiders come up from the south, if they were from further north?"

"To fool the local Indians, stupid! The raiders could stay hidden until the last minute, if they came around through Navy Channel."

"OK, OK," Rick agreed. "But one more problem. Your idea of a lookout on Dinner Bay would only work in the daytime. What if the raiders came at night?"

"OK, OK. You're being a spoil sport, Rick. The real raids were probably just before dawn. So *what*, if the kids could only play the game in daylight! But there's still one little problem I haven't solved."

"Only one?"

"What if that old cabin was built *before* Mr. Allen played his game? According to you, there were tons of white people on Mayne Island before he was born."

Rick nodded. "Grandfather Jones, my great-great-grandfather, he came here with his family in 1890. He and lots of other men cut logs to ship over to the new fish canneries near Vancouver, to heat their boilers." Rick stood up and peered intently at the old log cabin at the end of the bay.

"It's a tumble-down old shack, Dave. Could be very old. Maybe it was built even earlier, in the 1880s, by one of those men who settled here after he didn't find any gold in the Cariboo gold rush. There were quite a few of them."

"Or how about a deserter from the British Navy, or the American Navy?" suggested Dave. "Both of them were exploring and making maps around here in the 1850s. Mayne Island's named after one of the officers on a British survey ship, I think." Dave had learned more from Grandad's book than he'd realized. It had just slipped in through the cracks.

"Don't forget the Spanish," Rick added. "They were here too, maybe as early as the 1790s. You passed Galiano

Island when you came here on the ferry from Vancouver. That's a Spanish name. Could have been any of those sailors who were tired of sailing the seven seas. Before that, there were Russians, trading for the sea otter pelts. We could make that old cabin really old, if we keep trying!"

"But that's the problem," Dave said sadly. "If the cabin was there *before* Mr. Allen's childhood, then he wouldn't choose this hill. The view to the channel would be blocked. Wish I knew when that old place was built."

"There's your answer," said Rick, pointing down to the end of the bay.

Nine

"What do you mean, there's my answer?" asked Dave, shading his eyes to see where Rick was pointing. "Oh, that's just Mr. Sharp. It's not his cabin."

"He's lived here all his life."

"Yeah, come to think of it, Grandad told me that, but I wasn't really listening."

"Probably knows a lot about the cabin, at least. Let's zip over, eh Dave?"

Together they grabbed the Sitting Duck's small dinghy, its oars and a couple of lifejackets and were over at Mr. Sharp's dock in ten minutes. On the way, Dave asked Rick where *this* bay got its name.

Rick didn't know, but he guessed it might have something to do with so much food in its waters, a 'Dinner Bay Seafood Restaurant', in fact.

"Eat in, or take out," Dave suggested, "catering to seals, eagles, kingfishers, raccoons, otters and *people.*"

Mr. Sharp was getting ready to unload his own crab dinner, as they reached his dock. They waved at him as they glided in close.

"The old log cabin, eh, boys? Want to know its history?" he asked, easing himself down gently onto his rickety dock. "Set a spell, and I'll tell you. I only know what my old Pa told me. Built by Major McKenzie, that cabin was. I recollect Pa saying it was *after* the major came back from World War One. I think it was around 1919, or later."

The boys nodded to each other. That was all they really wanted to know, but it wouldn't be polite to leave too soon.

"Don't look like much now, do she?" said Mr. Sharp waving in the general direction of the cabin. "But Major McKenzie, he fashioned her in grand style, yessir! Cut the logs himself, but he imported special windows all the way from Seattle, no less. He died young. Fell off a log boom."

Mr. Sharp scratched his head and continued, "but before that, he and the missus had six daughters. Talk about noisy, they were the noisiest happiest family on the island. Youngest was in the same class as me. Hazel. We've had a school on Mayne Island since about 1883."

This guy's a living history book, thought Dave. He and Rick grinned at each other and stayed sitting on the dock, their feet dangling in the water. Mr. Sharp dozed off, and then woke with a start.

"Oh yes," he continued, " after the old Major died, and all the daughters married foreigners from the mainland, the widow loaned it to the Boy Scouts for as long as they wanted it." Dave nodded and began to fidget. This sounded like the beginning of yet *another* story.

"Yessiree!" said Mr. Sharp loudly. "Scouts had a

grand summer camp there, 'til the well ran dry. Then the widow gave the land to the Gov'ment, to be used for a park. They'll tear down the cabin soon, likely as not."

This could go on forever! thought Dave. "Excuse me, Mr. Sharp, I think my grandmother may be looking for us. We've got to go, but thanks a million! Hope your crabs are big ones."

They waved goodbye and headed for home. Dave didn't care about Major McKenzie, his six kids, his widow, or the Boy Scout camp. He didn't care what a grand cabin it had been when it was new. What he did care about was its absence.

"Yippee," he shouted, spraying Rick with the oars. "It wasn't there, back when Mr. Allen lived on the island! So, he could have been standing right where I want him to be. Maybe we should rename my grandparents' place Lookout Hill, instead of Reid's Roost!"

"Don't get too carried away, kid," suggested Rick, as he helped to stow the rowboat back on top of the sailboat. "Maybe you'd better wait 'til you check with Mr. Allen, tomorrow. You could be all wet, you know."

"I suppose his favourite game was baseball, even 'way back then," said Dave, kicking a rock.

"Aw, never mind," Rick said cheerily, "even if you're wrong, it makes a good story!"

Dave felt dejected. He'd put his heart and soul into solving the puzzle. Now Rick was throwing cold water on his ideas. He felt even more dejected when Rick announced that he had to get home.

Dave knew that the two of them had made a lot of headway this afternoon. They weren't just exchanging the time of day. They were actually listening to what the other had to say. Too bad it couldn't go on.

"I could come back for a while tomorrow," suggested Rick as they climbed the steps. "Maybe I could go along, when you visit Mr. Allen."

"Perfect," Dave breathed happily. "And we'd have time to see more of the shore along Navy Channel, maybe. Be great if we had a canoe. It'd be faster than the old rowboat."

"So, I'll bring my canoe, instead of my bike. See you in the morning," Rick yelled, as he picked up his bicycle and headed home.

Later on, when they were finishing dinner on the verandah picnic table, Gran had to ask Dave *twice* if he wanted more blackberry pie. He was still thinking about the log cabin that wasn't there. *Good name for a mystery story*, he thought to himself.

"Sorry, Gran, yes pie *and* ice cream, please." Maybe it was time to try his latest and greatest on the grandparents. They might be more enthusiastic than Rick had been.

"Hey, Gran, where's my letter to Susie? I want to show you the map I made on the back."

"Is that it, under Grandad's left shoe?" asked Gran calmly, as if that was where maps were always kept.

Dave rescued it and spread it out. "See, it's all connected with this low part at the end of the bay. It's hard to see 'cause of the heel mark." He took another bite of pie to give him strength, and scrubbed hard at the paper with his thumb.

"This got anything to do with the raiders from the north?" asked Gran, her eyes twinkling. "This boy gets his mental quirks from my side of the family!"

"Yes, Gran, *exactly*, raiders from the north, only they'd sneak in from the south, where they wouldn't be expected. Look here!"

Dave ran his finger along the raiders' route up Navy

Channel to Dinner Bay, and then around into Village Bay. "Do you follow me?"

Grandad nodded. Gran looked a little unsure. Patiently, Dave suggested that the attackers might have to wait in Dinner Bay for stragglers, or stall until it was the best time to attack.

"I'm getting worried about the Saanich People," said Gran, wringing her hands. "What they need is a good...."

"Lookout! *Yes*, Gran, exactly." Dave spent another five minutes going over his idea about a special lookout on this very hillside, and *then* ... Mr. Allen making up a game about it, years later. "It fits with the clues about Killer whales and the dangerous shape of Village Bay. Don't laugh. I could be right!"

Dave wanted so badly to convince them about Mr. Allen's game. It took him a few minutes more to explain about the log cabin being in the way, and the things he and Rick had learned about the cabin from Mr. Sharp. Gran looked happier now. At least she seemed to *half* believe Dave's scheme.

Grandad chuckled. "I can just imagine a young boy standing on this hill and then racing through the forest with a warning. How long would it take to Village Bay, straight through the forest? Mind you, Dave, I still think your idea's a little far fetched."

"Rick and I can time it tomorrow. He's coming back." Maybe then Gran and Grandad would believe him.

Susie would believe him. She'd believe *anything* Dave told her. He should finish his letter, now that he'd found it again.

"Hey, who put these blackberry fingerprints on my beautiful map?" he complained. "The shoe print's bad enough. Oh well, she's lucky to hear from me at all!"

He sat down at the picnic table and added the rest of his adventures, in large capital letters again, starting from the time he'd met Rick on the ferry, and then Mr.

Allen. It was mysterious, the way the new blackberry stains kept appearing on the crumpled paper. It was much better after he washed his hands.

When he finished, he sighed with relief and signed it,

YOUR ENTRIPID INVESTIGATOR,

DAVE

Oh, oh. He'd forgotten a few things. He found a second sheet of paper and added the extras:

P.S. .... HOW'S YOUR TONGUE TWISTER COLLECTION? AUNT MORNA SAID TO TELL YOU THIS ONE: TRY TYING TWINE TO TREE TWIGS! SAY IT THREE TIMES, FAST!

P.P.S. .... I CAN'T FIND AN INK ERASER. PLEASE FIX UP THE WORD ENTRIPID. I DIDN'T WANT TO MESS UP THIS NEAT LETTER BY SCRATCHING IT OUT. AND LOOK UP WIERD IN THE DICTIONARY. IT COULD BE WRONG TOO.

P.P.P.S. .... I'M OFFERING A PRIZE, OF I DON'T KNOW WHAT YET, IF YOU CAN FIGURE OUT WHAT THE FINGERPRINTS ON THIS LETTER ARE MADE OF. I'LL GIVE YOU A HINT, IT'S NOT BLOOD.

P.P.P.P.S. .... THE SHOE PRINT IS GRAN'S.
NO I'M KIDDING, HERS AREN'T THAT BIG.
IT'S GRANDAD'S!

BYE, SPOTTY, HOPE THE ITCHING'S
GONE. YOU'RE LUCKY IT'S NOT
SMALLPOX! SEE YOU SOON.

He got up from the table exhausted. For him, any kind of writing was a chore. "Just one more thing before it gets dark," he announced, and grabbed the *Case of the Careless Carpet Beetle*. Tucking it under his arm, he crept down the wooden steps one more time, determined to get close to at least one deer.

Seated behind the drooping Arbutus tree, he settled in. Evening was a good time to see deer. Maybe he'd be lucky. He often did two things at once. This evening he tried three.

Partly, he was following Alexandra, the fearless girl detective in the book, who was following the carpet beetle, who was following the....

Partly he was thinking about Mr. Allen. He'd forgotten to tell Rick about Mr. Allen's Indian name. Maybe he knew it already. If not, he'd tell him tomorrow. And partly, he was watching for....

All at once he spied them, only a few metres away. They appeared from nowhere, without a sound. The mother was picking her way daintily along the main trail that followed the edge of the cliff. Every few steps, she looked back, as if to check that the two fawns were following.

Dave could imagine the mother saying, "Now watch out, you two! Don't snap any twigs. Step where I step.

Just eat the soft green leaves, because the tough ones will give you a belly ache."

It was hard to stay still. Dave's left foot had pins and needles. He had to wiggle it without making a noise. He hardly dared to breathe, one fawn was so near. Their legs were as thin as ... chopsticks, with ... hinges in the middle. Their ears flicked back and forth and their dainty noses twitched, alert for signs of danger.

The fawn closest to him stopped suddenly, probably frightened by a chipmunk who was scampering along a fallen tree. The second fawn seemed braver. He appeared to be staring at a noisy blue Kingfisher who was diving into the bay.

The mother deer came back and gave the fawn a nudge. *Is she telling him to stay away from the water?* thought Dave.

Close by, a dog gave one short sharp bark. All three deer froze for a few seconds. Only their tails and noses and ears kept moving. Then, as quickly as they had arrived, they departed, straight up a steep trail that disappeared into a patch of blackberry bushes. Soon the three were completely out of sight.

"Wow! Was I lucky," shouted Dave to a passing woodpecker, as he ran up the steps. He hadn't expected to see deer as close as that.

"Here's an envelope for Susie's letter," said Gran, at the kitchen door, even before he had time to tell her his news about the deer.

"Oh, no! My letter's gone," he moaned, searching all around the picnic table where he'd left it. "After all that work!"

"If you left it outside," said Grandad, who was filling

the kitchen wood box, "Miranda may have taken it." Sure enough, after a few minutes of frantic searching, he found the pages under the verandah. Now the second page was torn, and the first page had raccoon prints, as well as the dark red blotches and the shoe marks.

"Got any sticky tape, Gran?" He mended the tear, stuffed both pages in the envelope and addressed it quickly before another calamity struck. Handing the letter to his grandmother, he asked her if she'd mail it tomorrow when she went to the store.

Oh no! That reminded him of something else. Taking Gran into a corner, he confessed about dropping the flashlight overboard the first evening, and his plan to buy a new one.

"Accidents can happen to anyone dear," she whispered. "Trouble is, none of our stores carry the right kind. I think Grandad needs one that floats, don't you? Phone your Aunt Morna. She can bring you one when she comes."

I almost struck out, thought Dave, *I've been so busy thinking about Mr. Allen's game and about making things right with Rick, everything else got forgotten.*

He realized that he'd even forgotten about moving to Chicago. *What do you know?* he told himself. *It's like I'm on another planet. Good, Grandad's going outside. Here's the number, 1-555-5450.*

"Hi, Aunt Morna? It's me, Dave. Could you do me a little favour?"

Ten

The next morning flew by. As soon as Rick arrived at seven-thirty they got busy. First, they tested the running time from the house to Village Bay. Avoiding the winding roads wherever they could, they chose rough trails through the forest. It took less than seven minutes.

Then, with their lifejackets on, they paddled Rick's canoe around to Navy Channel, to the low spot behind the log cabin. From there they raced to Dinner Point, across the mouth of Dinner Bay to Crane Point, and around that high headland to the beach at Village Bay.

Thirteen minutes hard paddling, with no stops. Great! So, a running lookout would have had time to warn the people in the village before the raiders arrived. That was exactly what Dave had hoped to prove.

Rick seemed to be enjoying himself. He admitted that

it was too bad when you felt too old to play games from your imagination. He still couldn't or wouldn't say that this could be connected to Mr. Allen's childhood game. They'd have to wait and hear it from the old man's own lips, wouldn't they?

"Now let's set your crab trap," suggested Dave, not wanting to waste a minute. They loaded it with a fish head, and dropped it from the canoe, not far from Grandad's dock. Later they could check to see if there were any crabs big enough to keep.

"These crabs have to be four and a half inches across," explained Rick, "or eleven and a half centimetres if your ruler is metric. And they should be male. The others we dump back in."

While they were out on the water, they slipped down to the end of the bay to check out the log cabin. Disappointingly, it was just an empty shell, where raccoons and squirrels had been living, rent free, for years. Nothing remained to connect it to the large and noisy McKenzie clan, or the Boy Scouts.

Back at Reid's Roost, the boys packed a lunch, borrowed some of Grandad's charts, and planned a much longer canoe trip. With any luck, they hoped to circle the whole island. This time they told Gran where they were going and when they'd be back, and they had to check the weather forecast and the times of the tides.

Canoeing beyond the nearby sheltered bays could be dangerous, if the wind or the tidal current was too strong. Dave knew that without being told. He'd seen the effects of both wind and tide already.

When they set off at last, they still had three hours before they were due to meet Mr. Allen. From Dinner Bay they went counter-clockwise, heading down Navy Channel for a start.

Rick pointed out his house halfway along the channel. Tomorrow they'd drop in. Today they wanted to go swimming instead. They beached the canoe in three different bays and tried each one. The last was the warmest. The tide, turning by now, crept in slowly over flat rocks that held the heat of the sun.

As they paddled between swimming spots, Rick told Dave about his Dad's orchard and beehives and the sheep that Rick helped to raise. Dave told Rick about his Dad's research about pollution in Lake Ontario.

Rick told Dave about his Aunt Jennifer, an electrical engineer in Montreal, and Dave told Rick about his two aunts, Aunt Morna who filmed sports news for the CBC, and Aunt Mary Jo, an operating room nurse.

Dave knew *her* even better than Aunt Morna, because she lived near them in Toronto. That was *another* reason why he hated the idea of moving. None of his relatives lived anywhere near Chicago.

Rick sympathized with him. He couldn't imagine moving, even as far as Vancouver. He had cousins on Pender Island, and his childhood friends close by. The boys kept right on talking as they rounded Georgina Point, and its landmark, a towering white lighthouse. Dave's arms and back were feeling the strain by now, but he wasn't going to admit that to Rick.

Paddling and eating their lunch at the same time, they chatted lazily about baseball and hockey. They even discussed girls, mainly about how they weren't crazy about them, at least not girls who chased them. By then, it was time to find Mr. Allen.

"That must be his friend's house," Dave decided, after they'd beached the canoe and scouted along the main road. "It's the only blue house on the hill near the church."

He was right. 'Nick Dominic', it said in faded letters on the mailbox. Mr. Allen must have seen them coming. He appeared at the front door, his finger to his lips.

"Shhh, the old boy's asleep," he warned. "Let's sit over there, under the apple tree." They settled down and

Mr. Allen leaned his back against the tree trunk. The only sounds were the rustling of the dry grass and the buzzing of the odd bee, as well as the gentle hum of ferries and smaller boats in the busy channel far below.

Mr. Allen explained that his friend was ninety-nine, and not as spry as he used to be. They'd been friends ever since World War One, when they'd spent two long and dreary years in a prisoner of war camp. They'd kept each other alive, with their songs and jokes.

"But let's talk about something else," he said to Dave. "Who's your friend, here?"

"You don't recognize me," said Rick, sounding disappointed. "Richard Jones, no relation to Dave. I live down on Navy Channel, and my Granny was your niece. Mary Paul. Remember her?"

"Reckon I do. And I reckon I saw you once, when you were little."

"I was four, and you scared me out of my *mind* with an old stone axe. Still got it?" asked Rick.

Mr. Allen laughed. "Family treasure. Hundreds of years old. Before we Indians had metal tools, we did everything with tools like that."

"Must have taken longer to cut down a tree," said Dave.

"Maybe ... two men ... two days, for a big one," guessed Mr. Allen. "Sometimes they'd burn it part way through first. Lucky for me, we had metal axes and cross cut saws, when I was building my house." He stopped to catch his breath.

"Mine's a Jim dandy log cabin," he continued. "Me and my brothers, we cut and peeled the logs and put it all together. Say, what have you been up to, since I saw you last, Dave? Lost any more bolts off your bicycle?"

"Mostly, I've been working on the clues you gave me."

"Figured them out yet?" asked Mr. Allen. He had an

impish smile, and Dave wondered whether he gave those same clues to other young visitors. Probably he enjoyed teasing, especially the easterners.

"Well, it's like this," Dave began, just as a ripe apple dropped off the tree and hit him on the shoulder. Mr. Allen reached over and grabbed the apple.

"Keep talking, Dave. You talk, I'll munch," he ordered.

Dave tried to speak slowly, thinking before each sentence. He was worried that something he said about the old time Indian raiders might offend Mr. Allen. You never knew what might upset other people, until it was too late. He'd learned that lesson the hard way.

The old man seemed to be listening, but it was hard to tell. Mostly, he just chomped on his apple, nodded his head and smiled a lot. Nothing that Dave said about the Indians in the old days seemed to be bothering him.

Once, when Dave was explaining his ideas about the childhood game, Mr. Allen stopped munching long enough to say, "Yes, that reminds me ... I was just twelve, the last summer we were on the island. And that's when my Dad made me a new stone scraper."

Great, thought Dave. *Now's my chance.* "What do you scrape, with a ..." he managed to say before Rick interrupted.

"I've seen lots of those stone scrapers in the museum in Victoria," Rick was saying. "And we've got some in our school collection. Was yours made from a river stone?"

"Yes," answered Mr. Allen in a shaky voice, "a special dark stone, tumbled smooth by a rushing river. From a river over on Vancouver Island, ours were. I can see those stones now." The boys had to bend close because Mr. Allen was speaking so softly.

"Yes?" Dave whispered. "Tell us about your own stone, the one you lost."

The old man looked confused, as if he wasn't quite sure where he was. He tapped his forehead and started talking again. "My Dad would hit the stone just right. It would split like magic. Edges were so sharp, you could scrape meat from a bone, or strip the bark off a stick."

"Hey," Rick said, "Granny used a stone scraper to take the outside skin off the camas bulbs, the non-poisonous ones, of course. She used to roast those bulbs for us. I loved them when I was a little kid."

"Me too," said Mr. Allen, smacking his lips. "You boys hungry? I think we *all* need an apple." He reached up to a low hanging branch for three more. That gave Dave a chance to ask another question.

"How big was your scraper?"

"Small enough to fit here," said Mr. Allen, pointing to the palm of his cupped hand. "Better than a Swiss army knife, for being useful. I was always peeling sticks. Carried that stone everywhere, until I lost it the last summer we were here."

"Why did you move away?" asked Dave.

"My Mom died that next winter. From tuberculosis, they said. After that, my two younger brothers and I, we stayed with my aunts and uncles over on Vancouver Island. Dad died on a canoe trip a month later, in a storm."

Dave wished he'd never asked. It was too sad to talk about. Mr. Allen shook himself and bit into his apple.

"Well, Dave," he said a moment later, "back to you. All that business about the raiders."

Oh no, Dave thought. *I was wrong. He's going to tell us his game was about something else.*

"You were right, dead right," said the old man with a wide grin. The boys grinned back. "We *did* play a game about raiders. Heard plenty of stories about them, yessirrie!"

Mr. Allen sat very still, but his eyes sparkled. Dave

guessed that he was reliving the old game, hearing the voices of his friends among the trees and across the water once again.

"You know, boys, there really was an Indian village there, right in the bay, before my time. Maybe it was just a summer fishing camp, maybe not. I've heard tell that the map makers from the British Navy showed it on their maps."

"When?" Dave thought it would be fascinating to look at the actual maps. "When were the maps made?"

"Probably around the 1850s, 1860s," Mr. Allen guessed, his wrinkled brow wrinkling even deeper. "By the turn of the century, the Indians were mostly over at the Helen Point Reserve, as far as I know."

So Village Bay really does make sense, Dave thought happily. *That's something. That's how all of this got started.*

"Congratulations, Dave," Mr. Allen was saying. "You solved the clues about Killer whales, and the dangerous shape of the bay, just like I hoped you would. I bet you feel good about *that!*"

Eleven

Yes, Dave did feel good. He felt great. That was partly because Mr. Allen seemed pleased that he'd solved the puzzle. Sometimes people don't *really* want you to guess their riddles. Maybe now he could risk one more question.

"How about the lookouts?" he asked cautiously. That was the part of the game that was most important. "Where did they...?"

"There was a hill," said Mr. Allen, his eyes narrowing to slits, "a hill where you could see the channel between Mayne Island and Pender Island. We always posted a lookout there. I expect that part of the island's covered with houses now."

"Would you recognize the hill if you saw it again?" asked Rick, sounding hopeful. Dave was glad that Rick had asked. He'd been afraid to ask the question, in case the answer was wrong. He could feel the butterflies in his stomach as he waited for the answer.

After a long pause, Mr. Allen said, "No, I wouldn't know the exact place. Such a long time ago and so many changes. And by the way, about my game, I hope you realize, the lookout on the hill was only good in the...."

"Daylight." Dave finished the old man's sentence.

"Actually," continued Mr. Allen, lowering his voice, "the real raiders probably travelled before first light, and attacked at dawn. At night, the lookouts would need to be right down on the shore of Navy Channel. We did that too, in our game. Even then, if it's a dark night, it's tricky spotting a canoe. A good paddler's a silent one."

"Yeah, we knew the lookout hill was just for the daytime. Well, Rick figured that part out," admitted Dave, grudgingly.

"Good for you, Rick. You two boys have taken me back ... my old friends and our game ... catching crabs for my Mom ... my Dad and the stone scraper...." Mr. Allen's voice trailed off to a husky murmur.

Dave had a sudden let down feeling. It would have been wonderful if Mr. Allen could have said that he'd been standing exactly where Reid's Roost stood now. But it didn't seem possible.

He could understand Mr. Allen not wanting to see that particular corner of the island. But it was sad, nevertheless. Now Dave would never know for sure about his special lookout hill.

Oh well, it wasn't the end of the world. There were other questions, about the present day.

"Mr. Allen," Dave began hesitantly, "about those canoes the Saanich People make nowadays, and the races. How long are those boats? And how many paddlers?"

"And when's the next race?" added Rick. "I was thinking I'd like to...."

"Slow down, boys," complained Mr. Allen. "Three questions all at once! Let's see, our biggest canoes are about fifty to sixty feet long, with up to eleven paddlers, and the next race is two weeks from Saturday, up at Cowichan Bay," he said in a rush, ticking off the answers on his knobbled fingers. Dave was already planning that he and Susie would go to a race next summer.

"Maybe I can get to the one in Cowichan Bay," Rick said eagerly. "I'd sure like to find out about a lot of things. I feel stupid not knowing much about my grandmother's, ummm ... my own relatives. I've got Saanich blood, even if I don't have an Indian name."

"Did Dave tell you mine?" Mr. Allen asked.

"No," admitted Dave, "I forgot. I'm still a bit confused about Indian names, but I remember yours." He traced it on the palm of his hand and up his arm. "Can I really call you by it?"

"Yes, of course. I was eight years old when I was named THAA,WEN. I earned it for working hard, helping the men unload the salmon from their canoes."

Dave could tell that THAA,WEN was proud of his name. You could hear it in his voice. "And you told me what it means too," Dave recalled. "It means coho salmon *and* the south end of Mayne Island, a double meaning."

"It's my name," Mr. Allen said proudly, "no one else's. Mine to pass on to one of my offspring. Billy, my eight year old great-great-grandson, maybe he'll earn it. At his school they teach the Saanich language and lots of things about our traditions. Remember, Dave, I showed you the little cedar canoe he carved."

"Getting an Indian name's not quite the same as getting stuck with any old name when you're born," said Dave, scratching his head. "I didn't have to do anything to earn mine."

Mr. Allen laughed. "No, it's definitely not the same. But sometimes you get called after one of your parents' favourite relatives. That's sort of special, eh? For both of us, a name giving's a great excuse for a party. We have a feast with drums and singing and dancing." He sat unmoving, his gaze far away. Neither Dave nor Rick urged him to talk.

Loud toots from two ferries far below brought them all back to the present. Mr. Allen checked his watch and struggled to his feet.

"Better get back to my old buddy, Nick," he said, leaning on Dave's shoulder for a moment. "And I'm delighted to meet you, again, Mr. Richard Jones, grandson of Mary Paul." He ruffled Rick's hair and shook his hand firmly.

"Well, stranger," he said as he took Dave's hand. "Glad your handlebars fell off. Otherwise we might never have met. Davey Jones, eh? Ever thought of being a salt water sailor when you're older? Or maybe a detective. You're already a champion puzzle solver."

"Thanks, ummm, Mr. Allen," mumbled Dave. He and Rick stood silent as Mr. Allen picked them two more apples each, waved his goodbye, and started toward the house. It seemed to Dave that he didn't want the boys to come any farther with him. He'd said all he wanted to say.

"Quite a guy," Rick remarked, as they made their way down the hill. "Bet you won't forget *him* in a hurry. THAA,WEN. I like that name. Hey, Dave, did you notice we still haven't got up the nerve to actually call him by it."

"Yeah, I felt badly about that," Dave had to admit. "But it still didn't seem right."

"Don't forget," Rick said firmly, "if you ever get another chance, don't forget the pause in the middle. Come on. Quit looking over your shoulder. We've got lots more to do this afternoon."

By the time they finally got back to the canoe, the two boys had covered a lot of territory, most of it up and down. Rick had insisted that there was plenty of time to explore the highest hill on the island.

Dave hadn't been too enthusiastic, but it was hard to argue with Rick. He seemed to assume that he was in charge. After all, it was his island.

When they reached the top of the hill, Dave was really glad that Rick had insisted. From their perch on some bare rocks, they could see for miles in every direction.

To the north, across twenty-five miles of sea, a line of jagged peaks marked the mainland of British Columbia. "The water between here and there is the Strait of Georgia," Rick explained. "It used to be called the Gulf of Georgia, and that's why this chain of islands is called the Gulf Islands."

"So that's why. I was going to ask somebody. Strange how the colours change," said Dave squinting at the ocean far below. "At sea level, it looked more greenish. From up here, it's blue, with a wrinkled skin. Looks like the hide of an elephant."

"You know, you're right," said Rick, sounding surprised. "And the tide and the gusts of wind are shifting the wrinkles."

"Neat!" said Dave, mesmerized.

Rick pointed across the strait. "See that smudge where the ocean meets the mountains? That's Vancouver. On a clearer day you could see some of the tall buildings."

"Yeah, Vancouver, where the airport is," said Dave in disgust. He'd have to fly home in a couple of days, like it or not.

"What's the matter?" asked Rick. "You look like you've lost your last friend."

"I will, when we move to Chicago. I didn't get a chance to tell you much about Nate and Thang and Jason, but I'll sure miss those three. We're together all the time."

"Quit belly aching, Dave! It's tough, but you'll make new friends. You've made two this week: me and the old man."

"So I did!" Dave brightened.

"And Chicago has two baseball teams."

"Right! The Cubs, and the White Sox. Yeah! Not as good as the Blue Jays, though. Hey, look down there, Rick. I can see three ferries, and some tiny specks, canoes or motor boats, I guess. See, even the little specks are leaving white trails on the blue skin. Like scratches that fade away behind them. Hey, neat!"

"Now look over your right shoulder, sort of south eastish," ordered Rick. "Those are the San Juan Islands, over in Washington State."

"I didn't realize we were that close to the American border."

"We are. The San Juans are part of the same island chain as the Gulf Islands. Take you maybe ... half an hour in a motor boat to get to the first big one. You have to call in at the American Customs dock before you go ashore."

"We're taking the sailboat down there next summer, my grandparents and my sister and me." Dave thought about next year. He knew these waters now, and he'd have to teach Susie about tides and beacons and marine charts.

Maybe next summer they'd be lucky enough to see a pod of Killer whales up close. Or at least some Harbour seals. So far, he'd seen only one shiny round seal's head. It had popped up like a jack-in-the-box, on the far side of Dinner Bay. At night, he'd heard seals barking once or twice.

"Turn around," Rick was saying. "If you shade your eyes, you can see the hills of Vancouver Island, to the west. Anybody tell you how big that island is? It's...."

"Two hundred and eighty miles, from top to bottom. If anybody else tells me that, I'll...." He gave Rick a friendly punch. "How come nobody tells me in kilometres? Hey, we ought to be heading home."

Their downward jogging route led straight through the bustling centre of island activity at Miners Bay. Hikers, bikers, cars *everywhere*. "No time now," panted Rick, pointing at a tiny building, "but that's the museum. Used to be the old jail."

"*Next* summer," said Dave, reluctantly, as they hurried down to the beach to retrieve the canoe.

Their homeward paddle took them along the densely wooded shore of the Helen Point Indian Reserve. "Next summer," sighed Rick, "I *promise* I'll find someone who knows more than *me* to take us hiking through there."

"My grandmother had the same idea," Dave said. "Yesterday she phoned all *over*, trying to find someone who lived there, or even knew much about it. Seems half the island's away fishing this week."

It's good and it's bad that there's never enough time, he thought to himself. *It means there's always something left to explore.* He rubbed his sore shoulders. They'd paddled a long way, he and Rick, and they weren't home yet.

Luckily the tide was slack now, because the passage through the narrows near the tip of Helen Point could be tricky in a canoe. The water usually came through in a great rush, in one direction or the other. Even at slack tide there were whirlpools that looked threatening.

It was just here, that first evening, that Dave and Aunt Morna had tangled their fishing lines with the ones in the next boat. And it was between Helen Point and Crane Point that Dave had lost the flashlight.

Some fish at the bottom of the sea probably had a big surprise, thought Dave with a smile, as he paddled on.

It was seven o'clock by the time they'd completed the

circle back to Dinner Bay, and Rick had to dash off home. "You keep the crabs," Rick shouted as he skimmed off into the distance.

Using the rowboat, Dave pulled in the trap and let two small crabs escape. Three fierce ones were big enough to go into a pail and up to the kitchen. "Ouch!" He sucked his sore finger. He'd forgotten his mother's warning. That biggest one sure could bite!

He got his chance to bite back, when he and his grandparents ate their mouth watering Dinner Bay Take Out. Then he sprawled on the sofa, determined to finish his mystery book. Of course he knew how it ended. *The Careless Carpet Beetle* got squashed by the *criminal*, but he liked the story even better the second time. There was something very satisfying about tying up all the loose ends.

The final loose end tied, at ten o'clock he announced that he was heading for bed. Tomorrow would be his last day, and Rick had promised to come back early. They were planning to go to Rick's place, find a few friends and have a baseball game.

Rick might have time to teach me some new sailor's knots too, and who knows what else! Maybe Grandad would take them both for a sail. Tomorrow would tell.

Twelve

"Beep .... Beep .... Beep."
The faint but regular sound was the first thing Dave
heard next morning. He tried to guess the time between
beeps. *Sort of one every twenty seconds?*

When he checked it with his watch, yes, he was
exactly right about the timing. So, it must be the fog horn
on Lighthouse Island. He'd looked it up in Grandad's
Coast Guard book when they'd had their picnic in Lighthouse Bay.

He ran to the window, but all he could see was a thick
grey blanket that smothered everything. Just faintly, he
could hear the water lapping against the unseen shore.
There seemed to be no wind this morning. No trees
rustled. The fog hid even the closest tree from his sight.

That cedar tree had been on his mind almost before he

woke up. It was huge, a giant sunshade, shielding the house and the smaller trees and bushes. A tree like that must be really old. What if....

His thoughts were interrupted by the sudden crash of waves on the invisible rocks below. Sitting Duck's wire rigging rattled with a familiar tinkle. And now he could hear other sounds, loud thumping ones. Perhaps it was the steep metal ramp, as it banged on top of the floating dock?

Next, the Boom ... Boom ... Boom of a deeper fog horn seemed to be competing with the little beeps from the fog horn at the lighthouse. What was happening?

It was hard to imagine what it would be like in Dinner Bay, or farther out in the open water. Like potato soup?

Cold potato soup. The air was decidedly chilly, even with no wind. You wouldn't go out there without a good reason.

It would be even more scary than the night he'd lost the flashlight. At least he'd been able to see where the water ended and the shore began, just barely. But what was causing all the commotion out there? What had made the waves start up?

Maybe the waves were bow waves from a big ship. On a calm day those waves were very noticeable when they reached the shore. Probably the ship that was making the waves and the loud booms was a ferry. Dave was sure *he* wouldn't want to be a ferry Captain. *No thanks!* Even with radar, it wouldn't be fun.

When the excitement seemed to be over, he decided that he might as well get dressed and rustle up some breakfast. He'd slept in and it was ten-thirty. Rick hadn't come after all. Hardly surprising. Maybe after the fog lifted.

He was just about to crack an egg or three, when a new ship started its deep sounding booming, and then a second one with a slightly different tone. The two different sounds came from the same spot, or so it seemed. Dave ran to the verandah. The soup was as thick as ever.

The next sound he heard was a series of blasts, five of them. It sounded like a ship's regular signal, not its eerie fog horn. Five blasts meant, "Look out, you're standing into danger!" What was going on out there?

A few minutes later, came the sound he was least expecting. Someone was clattering up the ninety-nine steps as if his life depended upon it. It couldn't be Grandad. He wasn't crazy enough to have gone fishing in the fog. Anyway, he couldn't run that fast.

"Dave? You there?" came a weak voice from below.

"Rick? Is that you? Your voice sounds funny."

"Ferry boat nearly scared me into ... next week! Gave me five blasts! He was 'way off course ... after ... shifting to miss ... *another* ferry!"

"Wow! Hey, I never expected you to come in the canoe, in this fog!"

By now, Rick was nearing the top of the steps, and he was almost out of breath. "Should have ... known better," he puffed. "Dad'll probably give me a lecture, but ... thought it would be calm all the way, if I ... followed the shore. Faster than ... biking, from ... my place. Besides ... down at water level ... not so bad."

"Really, Rick? You got x-ray vision?"

Rick collapsed by the kitchen door, and said nothing for a few moments. "X-ray vision!" he repeated, finally. "Matter of fact, I lost my glasses when the ferry tooted me. My distance sight is lousy. But if you stick close to the shore, and listen, you're OK."

"Hmmmm," Dave said, "I suppose you can hear the water slapping the rocks, and guess your way along. Come on in, Rick. Hot chocolate? Cinnamon bun?"

"Sorry. Have to go back. Thought I'd see if you

wanted to come and help me, since I landed up at your dock, anyway. When I came around Dinner Point from Navy Channel, I thought I heard someone crying. I'm still not sure if it was animal or human."

"Weird!"

"Well, I was just heading ashore to take a look, when I got all tangled up with the big ships. Almost capsized! It was just luck I ended up here. By then I didn't know *where* I was. Coming to help me check this out, Dave?"

"Sure!" Dave grabbed his sweater and was starting down the hill before he thought about telling his grandparents. He was *almost* positive they wouldn't stop him. After all, it was an errand of mercy. And he'd be with Rick, and Rick was so ... dependable.

Anyway, it wasn't far across the bay, was it? He'd put his lifejacket on, and take Grandad's loud whistle.

But he knew he should let the grandparents know where they were going. He shouted twice, but no answer. It was strange, because the car was still in the driveway. He scribbled a quick note and left it where they'd find it, on the door mat with a stone on top.

10:45 A.M. GONE WITH RICK IN HIS CANOE. HEADING TO DINNER POINT. RESCUE MISSION. DON'T WORRY! D.J.

Down at the dock, Dave grabbed his lifejacket from the sailboat. Rick hadn't taken his off.

"Hang on a sec," shouted Dave, as Rick started to get into the canoe. "Let's leave the light on, the sailboat's masthead light. It might help us when we're coming back."

"Good thinking, Dave. Now hop in," ordered Rick. "You paddle in front, and me in back. You're the lookout, since I lost my glasses."

They slipped away from the dock before Dave had time to think too carefully about what lay ahead. When he'd wakened to the sound of the fog horn's beeps, he certainly hadn't expected to be out in Dinner Bay, heading for....

"How'll we know where to go?" Dave asked. "I can't see the other side at all."

"We'll go all the way round the bay, even if it takes longer. That way we'll be sure to pass the place where I heard the noise."

"Sounds good to me!" Dave's secret fear had been that they would end up out in that open water beyond Dinner Point, and meet a ferry, as Rick had done earlier. Dave was sure he would panic. *Then* what would Rick think of him?

"Now listen for the waves breaking on the rocks," warned Rick, "and keep your eyes peeled, right where the water and the land meet. Tell me when we pass Mr. Sharp's dock. There's a submerged rock just past there."

"Ha! This reminds me of my first night on Mayne Island, when I went fishing with Aunt Morna," Dave said, through his clenched teeth. "Here I am, again, listening for my life, and keeping my eyes peeled. Later, I'll tell you about the fish I caught, when we're not so busy. Whoops! We almost tipped!"

"We're going through a patch of bull kelp," said Rick holding up a rubbery round blob with a six foot long rat tail attached. "That means it's fairly shallow. We're down at the end of the bay now. What's that ahead, Dave? It's a bit blurry."

"Motor boat at anchor, and next it's Mr. Sharp's dock. Yes, there are his crab traps piled on the end. OK, so far. We'll be past the underwater rock in a minute. *Now* can we head a little closer to the shore?"

"Yeah, kid, but take it easy. You could put a hole in this old canoe in two seconds. Leave a bit more room between us and the shoreline!"

"*I know, I know.* Hug the shore, don't kiss it. I'm getting lots of practice!"

"Shh. From now on, let's just listen for any kind of sound. The one I heard was more like a squeal than a cry."

"OK, Rick." They paddled in silence for another five minutes or more. Dave wished that *he* had x-ray vision, to pierce the shroud that still imprisoned the bay. He could see about an arms length in front, and to the sides. Beyond that ... nothing. Where would this morning's adventure end up?

He wasn't afraid for his life. He had his lifejacket zipped up, and he was sure they wouldn't drown. But would this be an adventure he'd live over again in bad dreams? Suppose they found ... he didn't even want to think *what* it would be. He was cold in spite of his old turtleneck sweater.

"What's that?" Rick hissed. "I'm sure I heard something!"

Dave stopped paddling and stared hard at the dim cliffs that loomed over his left shoulder. "You must be dreaming, Rick. I didn't hear anything. Wait, I see something, though. Fog's lifting a little. Something small, right at the edge of the water. It's limping along. Could be a small raccoon. Thought I saw one catching crabs along here yesterday."

"Or it could be an otter," whispered Rick. "Do you suppose that's what I heard crying? It'll probably run away if we get any closer. But we should have a look. It might be injured. Find a good place to pull in."

"Pull in?" Dave thought Rick must be kidding. How could he pull in on this rocky shore? It was like that murky night with Aunt Morna, when she'd expected him to find the way home. He wasn't a magician.

Too bad Rick wasn't the front paddler. Too bad Rick had lost his glasses. How could Dave possibly land the canoe?

But at least he could try. Lately, he'd been doing a lot of unusual things. The worst that could happen was that he'd put a hole in Rick's canoe.

He inched closer to the cliff. Through the fog he could just barely see it rising steep and solid beside him. He could even touch it with his paddle. There was no way to land along this....

Wait a minute. Was that...? Yes it was: a small space between two huge boulders. Maybe in there, they'd find a place to land, if he could just steer the canoe through the opening. Rick was calling out in alarm, as Dave started to swing sharply to the left. Dave should have warned him.

Once they were in between the rocks, they were more protected from the force of the current out in the bay. But there was no room to use the paddle. Instead, Dave reached out to the rocks on either side and used his hands to push them along.

Rick did the same. They were making progress. Now if Dave could only spot somewhere to beach the canoe.

Was that a speck of gravelly beach up ahead? Wonderful! Gently, he grounded the bow of the canoe and hopped ashore. Well, at least they'd got this far. Now what?

"Good job, Dave!" whispered Rick. "Now let's keep our voices down, and have a look." They pulled the canoe up on the gravel, and then headed back over the rocks and through the thick undergrowth, towards the spot where they'd seen the small animal.

Dave was sure that it would have scuttled away by now. Wild creatures don't wait around to welcome strangers.

"Stop," ordered Dave. His stomach churned. They both stood still and waited.

There it was again, almost a moaning sound. To Dave it sounded like a little....

"Yes, it is," Dave called back to Rick. "I can see him now. It's not an otter or a raccoon. It's a just a *puppy*, for heavens sake!"

"Must have wandered down from one of those houses away up in the forest," Rick guessed. "Couldn't find his way back. Even if we catch him, we'd never find our way up there in this weather."

Or through these blackberry bushes, thought Dave. He'd already been thoroughly scratched. "Why don't we take him back to our place? Come here, puppy, we won't hurt you."

"He's shivering," said Rick, after Dave had finally caught hold of the whimpering bundle of brown fur and placed him in Rick's arms. "Gee, Dave, he's cute, now that I can actually see him."

"I don't think he's hurt, just lost," Dave decided. "Here, Rick, wrap him in my sweater. On the way back, you can sit in front with the puppy, and I'll paddle."

Dave realized that somewhere along the way, it was he who was making the decisions. He was sorry that Rick had lost his glasses, but it certainly had put Dave on the spot. Now it was as if he'd passed some kind of test. It felt good.

With Rick and the puppy behind him, he lead the way back to the canoe. Fortunately, the fog was lifting quite noticeably at water level, and it was much easier to see the way home.

As they got close to the dock, the masthead light of the *Sitting Duck* acted like a beacon. Carefully, Dave paddled in behind the sailboat, and gently, Rick carried his blue bundle up to the house.

"Grandad can feed the puppy and I'll feed the boys," announced Gran, after they'd burst inside, shouting news of the rescue. "All three of you look like you're starving. Incidentally, Dave, thanks for leaving the note. We were just next door, having coffee. Grandad and I knew you'd be OK."

Dave thought that was very optimistic of her. There were a few times when he hadn't been so sure.

"Is wool good for a puppy?" asked Grandad. "This one's eaten half of Dave's sweater! Maybe he'll settle for some of my sausages."

"Hot tea, lots of sausages and buttermilk pancakes, that's what you boys need," declared Gran, stirring some pancake batter. The boys toasted themselves by the kitchen's black Monster, while they watched the puppy.

The little fellow attacked his sausages and then tore around the kitchen yapping and tumbling playfully. He seemed none the worse for his adventures.

He was a cocker spaniel, no more than two months old, and his fur was the colour of sultana raisins. It was nearly dry now, and as soft as the fluff on a dandelion.

The problem was that he still preferred *anything* made of wool. It was too bad about Grandad's woolen socks that had been drying beside the stove. Gran kept a wary eye on the puppy while the boys ate.

Dave was sorry to see that Rick had emptied the last drop of the Real Ontario Maple Syrup onto his leaning tower of pancakes. *Oh well*, he sighed to himself, *next year I'll bring the giant size bottle.*

"By the way, was that *lunch?*" Dave asked anxiously, when they'd finished everything in sight. The kitchen clock said twelve-thirty. "I slept in, and Rick came before

I even *started* breakfast. I'm pretty full, but I think I could squeeze in an apple. Hey, how about those chocolates?"

There were only a few left. Generously, Dave offered them first to Rick.

"Rick and I need lots of energy," he announced. "Rick doesn't know it yet, but he's going to help me. There's something I've been meaning to do, ever since I woke up."

"I'm too tired, Dave," said Rick, as he pushed himself away from the table wearily. Dave could sympathize. After all, Rick had been out on *two* adventures in the fog, first the near collision with the ferry, and then the rescue of the puppy.

Still, this was important. Dave grabbed Rick by the shoulders and pleaded with his eyes.

"OK, kid," Rick agreed grudgingly. "I owe you one. But, for heaven's sake, what ever it is, let's get it over with. The puppy's fine, but I'm zonked!"

Thirteen

"It's like this," Dave said desperately, after he'd dragged Rick outside. "See that big cedar? Well, this morning in the fog, I had another brain wave about THAA,WEN. It was like his voice was sort of ... calling me, from across the bay. Quit laughing, Rick!"

Rick stopped laughing and looked mad instead. "What about the old cedar tree?" he said, kicking a stone.

"Well, how old is it? That's all I want to know."

"Couple of hundred years, at least," decided Rick, after he'd tried to put his arms around the scarred old trunk. "This one's seen a lot of summers."

"Well ... remember not to laugh, but suppose they were looking for a tree to climb. Why wouldn't they...."

"You mean THAA,WEN and his friends? Aw, come on, Dave, that's going too far! The forest's full of big trees.

Even more, away back then, before people logged off the biggest ones. He could have climbed any one of hundreds, if he climbed a tree at all." Rick flopped on the ground, looking tired and disgusted.

"*Anyway*," Rick went on, his cap pulled down over his eyes, "he never *said* he climbed a tree, did he? Gee, Dave, we're talking about a silly game, not something real!"

"You mean ... real, like rescuing puppies?"

"Yeah, well that kind of thing, something important. I'm getting tired of your puzzles, Dave."

"Yesterday you said it was fun."

"Well, that was yesterday. Hey, *wait* a sec!" Rick was looking really upset now. "Why do I have this stupid feeling you actually want me climb that tree? It's got no side branches at the bottom. Can't be done, unless you get some loggers' boots."

"We could...."

"No, we couldn't. Anyway, I ought to get home and help my Dad mend some fences. Take my advice, Dave," Rick said, frowning. "You're in some kind of fantasy land. Live in the real world! 'Bye, Dave. I've got to go."

"Pleeeease, Rick, don't go yet. You saw the old guy, yesterday. You know he's real. He's your grandmother's uncle, isn't he? I've never met a more real... character, in my whole life! I just want to tell him that I tried this one last idea, even if it is crazy. He'll get a laugh out of it." Rick shrugged his shoulders.

"Aw, come on," Dave pleaded. "It'll only take a few minutes! And don't tell my grandmother, will you? She'd have a fit. I'm not afraid of heights, and I've figured out how to do it. Come on, Rick, you're going to help!"

"No way! Climbing's okay for raccoons and squirrels, but not for this *boy!* I'm serious, Dave. I'm not climbing any old trees." Rick had a look of terror on his usually calm face.

102

"It's not the Empire State Building, Rick. It's only a...."

"You don't get it, do you?" Rick said sadly. "Most people have something they're afraid of. For me it's heights. I can't even watch when someone *else* is climbing. *No!* You're on your own on this one."

"But all I need is some help. I'm going to...."

"But, but ... I lost my glasses, remember," Rick protested weakly.

"Who cares! You don't need glasses just to steady the *ladder!* Keep your eyes closed, if you want. If I could just get up to that first big side branch. From there on, it's a breeze."

While he was talking, Dave was already dragging the heavy extension ladder from its place under the verandah. "Aw, come on, Rick! It won't take long!"

Finally, Rick gave in. They extended the ladder to its full length and planted it firmly against the rough cedar trunk. Rick braced himself and held on with both hands, his eyes tightly shut.

"You know," said Dave cheerily, as he started up, "For me it's snakes. That's what gives me the creeps." The ladder shook as he climbed, and he nearly lost his balance when two startled squirrels, startled *him.*

Fortunately, the squirrels had a choice. They could scurry around to the far side of the trunk. Next, a woodpecker scolded him, as if to say, "That's *my* tree!" Dave felt more and more unsure. Maybe this was one gigantic *mistake.*

As soon as he had his arms around the first fat side branch, he felt much better. His dizziness was going away. He rested for a moment. He'd been telling the truth about being afraid of snakes. But he was even more afraid of ladders. He usually managed to block it out of his mind, if the ladder was short.

He hated anyone to know. At home, his friends

teased him, but he couldn't help it. It wasn't the same as Rick's fear. It was sillier. It wasn't the height that bothered him, it was the wobble. He'd fallen off a rickety ladder when he was six, and he'd avoided them ever since.

Today, however, a little dizziness and a queasy stomach seemed like a small price to pay. He needed to climb this tree, this *very* tree. It was as if an unseen force was urging him on. *Guess I've got a certain person on the brain.*

"Come on, kid!" Rick sounded impatient. "You gone to sleep?"

"I'm on my way," called Dave. "The rest will be easy!" He scrambled from one strong branch to another. Once, he stopped to check out a hole that could have been a bird's home. No birds. Not even a nest. *Too late in the season for babies,* he decided.

He noticed an odd shaped stone wedged securely inside the empty hole, half blocking the entrance. *Strange place for a stone,* he thought idly, as he began to climb higher.

Soon he reached a natural stopping place. It was a flat spot on a huge limb. Probably the same place the raccoons often chose to rest. Dave could see where they'd scratched the branch. There was even room to lie down quite comfortably.

Lying on his stomach and leaning on his elbows, he gazed out at Dinner Bay, far, far beneath him. It was a miniature world. The tops of smaller trees, the roofs of houses ... like the view from a helicopter. His viewpoint wasn't as high as the hill he and Rick had climbed yesterday, but it was high enough.

This was THAA,WEN's lookout place. It couldn't have been better. Even in the distance, you could see every....

Only a few wisps of fog still hung on the tops of the trees, like hazy strands of Christmas tinsel. Several eagles wheeled silently, high in the sky. At the very end of Dinner Point, he caught sight of a pair of seals basking on the rocks, the same spot where they'd rescued the puppy.

At last, he'd seen seals out of the water. He could see that their coats were mottled and shiny. He wished he'd brought binoculars. Maybe next year, in the sailboat, he'd see seals even closer. And whales too, if he was lucky.

He heard voices down below. They were real voices this time. It was his grandparents, and it looked as if they were taking the puppy in the car. Probably going to look for the owner.

Good! I'll be down before they even know I've been up! he thought. He shifted around again, and faced the bay. Rick was wrong if he thought this wasn't the real world. Everything about it was alive, from the soaring eagles to the fish in the deepest part of the bay.

On and off all day he'd been thinking that climbing this tree would bring him closer to THAA,WEN. He was so sure that this was his lookout tree. Maybe the voices of the children from long ago would be easier to hear in this special place.

The old scraper THAA,WEN had lost.... It had been rattling around in Dave's mind, ever since the old man first mentioned it. Now that Dave had heard the whole story, he knew it was just a stone. Split and sharpened, but of no great value. Another one could be made in a short time. The value was that THAA,WEN's father had made it especially for him.

Dave remembered how terrible he'd felt when he'd lost the model sailboat that Aunt Mary Jo had made for him. It was too much to hope that Mr. Allen's stone would ever be found after all these years.

But just maybe, while Dave was up here in the cedar tree, he'd get some kind of inspiration. Like, some place to dig. Maybe twenty paces from a special rock on Village Bay beach, for instance. Like a pirate's treasure.

Suddenly Dave remembered poor old Rick waiting

patiently below. *I'd better go down,* he decided, reluctantly. But first he had to have one last look past the log cabin, and pretend. From this height, the cabin only partly blocked his view.

Hmmm.... It's a long time ago, hundreds of years before THAA,WEN*'s time. Not a single white person on the island, yet. I'm one of the Saanich People watching that low spot near the end of the bay. No cabins. Nothing.*

Dave's eyes narrowed. It was the same day dream he'd had many times, but this time it felt different.

Look, there's a canoe, twenty men in it, slipping stealthily by, on its way to raid the fishing camp. I'll have to go warn them! Here come six more. If I run fast, I'll be there in ... seven minutes. Better add two more, to get down this tree. Nine minutes. Hey! We timed the raiding canoes at thirteen minutes. That's running it a bit close!

He leaned far out. He could see Rick resting beside the tree. He looked like a toy, a limp rag doll.

"Hey, Rick!" he yelled. "This is it! The perfect place. I can see ... the whole world! Look out below. I'm coming down!" He left his safe perch and started on his way, craning his neck to chose each new foothold. For Rick's sake, he felt he should hurry, but it was much harder than going up.

As he passed the hole in the tree where he'd noticed the stone, he wrenched it out of its hiding place and stuffed it in his back pocket without looking at it. He'd add it to his rock collection. It puzzled him how it had got in the hole in the first place.

His stomach started to feel woozy again, as soon as he put his right foot on the top rung of the ladder. *If I go faster, it'll be over,* he decided. That was a mistake. Half way down, he missed his footing.

"Look out!" he shouted in a panic. "Look out below!"
Crash!
He fell to the left, just missing Rick, who had been

doing his best to keep the ladder against the tree. He *didn't* miss a prickly patch of blackberry bushes. He landed right in the middle.

To make matters worse, after he'd freed himself from the bushes, he stumbled and hit his head on a sharp rock.

"Ouch!" He couldn't help saying it. His knees and forehead were cut and bleeding, and his shoulder was aching badly.

"Now you've done it, you goofy kid!" scolded Rick. "Wait'll your grandparents get a load of this! What do you bet, they'll think it was my idea!"

"We've got time. Don't worry!" said Dave. "Help me get inside. I can get patched up before they get back." He was thinking about how Aunt Morna had fooled them when her hand was cut. He knew just where to look for the bandages.

But it was too late.

By the time the boys got to the kitchen door, a car was pulling into the driveway. "You and Rick been having a fight?" asked Grandad, as he struggled in with the groceries and caught sight of Dave. "Hope your Mom doesn't faint when she sees you tomorrow."

Gran looked as if *she* might faint, but she didn't, just dropped a dozen eggs on the floor instead.

Aunt Morna arrived just then. She threw Dave a towel to stop the bleeding over his eye, and started wiping up the trail of blood on the kitchen floor, while Rick tried to clean up the broken eggs.

So far, Gran had said nothing at all. She just smiled weakly and started to wash Dave's cuts. *Lucky she loves me,* he thought guiltily.

"Well," said Aunt Morna, sounding quite matter of

fact, as she helped with the bandages, "Looks like my fishing pal's had quite a holiday! I saw your sweater on the floor, all torn. And those shorts look ready for the rag bag!"

Dave explained about the puppy they'd rescued. It was really the puppy's fault about the sweater. As for the shorts, "well, that's a long story," he confided, as he checked his pockets. "I'll tell you in a minute. Here, Aunt Morna, you hang onto this old stone, while I go change. Look at the shape of it. It's weird!"

Fourteen

"You're right, this stone is weird!" said Aunt Morna when Dave came back. "See, it's sharp on the edge and one side's flat, and the other side's rounded. Where did you find it?"

"In a hole in the big cedar, halfway up." He took it back from her, and ran his fingers along the sharp edges. He was beginning to get a prickling feeling at the back of his neck. He handed the stone to Rick, and they both looked at it, wordlessly.

After everything that's happened, this would be the final touch, thought Dave. He clenched his fists so tightly that they ached. If only it could be true.

"It's a very dark grey," Rick said slowly, turning it over and over in his hand. "*Hey!*" After a long pause, he said quietly, "Are you thinking what I'm thinking Dave? I think this is...."

"Let me tell. It was me that found it," Dave said sharply, grabbing the stone and cradling it in his palm. Then he remembered that he couldn't possibly have climbed that cedar tree by himself. Not without Rick there to support the ladder.

Dave looked at his friend, patient, helpful, exhausted Rick. "No, I'm wrong," Dave said quietly. "We both found it. You tell, Rick." Now it was almost as if Dave didn't want to say what he was thinking. After all, it was too impossible.

"No, Dave, you're the nosy one," Rick teased. "Tell them what it is. Go on!"

"A scraping tool," said Dave, his voice cracking. "Like the ones the Indians used, for...."

"They used them for scraping meat from the bone," said Gran, "and the edible parts from plants, and for peeling sticks. I've seen scrapers like that in the museum."

"And now *we've* got one!" said Dave, waving the stone, "And guess who this one belongs to?" He was feeling braver all the time. Now he was almost *sure* he was right.

"The old man, THAA,WEN!" shouted Rick. "That old stone belongs to him!" Rick sounded as if he were totally convinced. "Yes," he added, looking very serious, "this is the very scraper he lost, the last summer he played his lookout game on the island. Isn't it Dave?"

If Rick was *that* sure, it must be true. "Yes, folks," Dave announced dramatically, "this is the very scraper he was talking about! Split from a river stone. See, Gran, doesn't this look like a river stone?"

Gran took it in her hand, and looked *through* her glasses this time, instead of over the top. "River stones are usually rounded like this, from being tumbled. And I've seen lots of dark grey ones. Goodness gracious, boys! This could be a genuine historical discovery!"

"Are you sure you don't mean hysterical?" asked Grandad, with a chuckle. "I'm kidding! It looks like a scraping tool to me. And it's sharp enough. But what was it doing away up in the cedar tree?"

"Too heavy for a small nesting bird to carry," said Aunt Morna. "They sometimes steal small shiny things. But stones?"

"And a squirrel certainly wouldn't store it for the winter," added Gran.

Dave was exploding. He had to tell them, whether they believed him or not. "Isn't it obvious?" he began bravely. "Mr. Allen, THAA,WEN, left it there himself, when he was twelve years old. He told me he didn't remember where he'd lost it. But he was sorry, because his Dad had made it for him."

The adults looked totally unconvinced, even his old fishing pal, Aunt Morna. Dave felt awful. He *so* wanted them to believe him. What more could he say?

Rick tried to explain. "You see, Dave wasn't climbing that tree just because he's a loony! He was hoping it was Mr. Allen's lookout place. When he got up to the raccoon's roost, the view was fantastic. He could see Navy Channel perfectly."

"Well now that we've found the stone," declared Dave, "we're even *more* sure about the lookout place, aren't we Rick?"

"You should call the old guy," suggested Rick. "Look up his grandson's phone number on Salt Spring Island. Dad knows him. I think it's S. Stanley, on Sunset Road. Hurry!"

Dave tried, but Mr. Allen was off fishing, and probably wouldn't be back before Dave had to leave for Vancouver. Dave didn't really want to do it, but he explained the whole story to the grandson, who sounded not at all impressed.

But he *did* promise he'd tell his grandfather all about

it. He gave Dave Mr. Allen's address on Vancouver Island, so that Dave could write to him.

Dave hung up the phone, feeling sad. It would have been great to talk to THAA,WEN and tell him the details in his own words. *And* to see his reactions. Since he was a great teller of tales, he'd appreciate a good story, even if it wasn't true.

Dave *did* have to leave the island this evening. August, and the summer holidays were almost over. Time to get on home and face whatever September would bring. Too bad he'd still have these bandages when he got home. Maybe Gran should phone his parents and warn them.

But it would be great to see them, and to tell everybody back home about Mayne Island, and everything that had happened. Day after tomorrow, Nate and Thang and Jason were coming over for lunch, and Dad was taking them all to a baseball game. That was something to look forward to.

And *maybe*, just *maybe*, after they got moved to Chicago, there'd be time to go to another game. Weren't the White Sox getting a new pitcher? He'd been so busy lately, he'd forgotten to read the sports pages.

He smiled to himself. He'd learned a lot this week, some of it about making friends. It wasn't so hard.

Part of what he'd learned was about himself, like how to slow down and listen, and try to see the other person's side. It seemed to work out better that way.

He thought about his parents and the plans to move to Chicago. Dave had been so *un*enthusiastic. He must have spoiled it for them. He felt differently about it now. Wait until he got back to Toronto, he'd try to....

"What's the matter dear?" asked his grandmother. "One minute you look like the world's coming to an end, and the next minute, you look like it's just beginning."

"Exactly," said Dave, deliberately not trying to explain. He looked at his watch. "Time I got packed," he declared.

He and Rick hurried off to collect Dave's 'collection'. Apart from the precious scraper tool, which he and Rick had already decided should be sent to THAA,WEN, the other things were still down by the twisted Arbutus tree where he'd stored them.

There was a blue Kingfisher's feather he'd found floating in the bay, a purple starfish he'd pulled off a rock, a dozen assorted beach stones and shells, and some crab claws, left behind by an eagle, perhaps.

His finger still hurt where the crab had nipped him yesterday. Yes, his mother was right. You had to be careful taking them out of the trap.

When he had everything in a pile in the living room, Grandad held the red back pack open, while Dave stuffed it.

"Phew!" said Grandad, plugging his nose at the dirty socks and the purple starfish. "They may not let you on the plane! Say, Dave, how come your pack's lighter than when you came?"

Dave had been wondering about that too. "I guess we ate all the chocolates and the Maple Syrup, my shorts are in the rag bag, and that wreck of a sweater's not worth taking home."

"Another ten minutes and I'll have this one finished," said Gran, knitting furiously on his purple, green, yellow, red, white and black one. "When you wear it, Davey dear, you'll remember that first evening when it put you to sleep!"

"And my new friends will be able to find me in a crowd," he said giving her a quick hug.

"Right now," announced his aunt, holding a paper bag in the air, "it's surprise time!" Dave knew immediately what was inside the bag. He pounced on it and ran off to get the money he owed Aunt Morna.

Now he was ready to hand the mystery bag to Grandad. But where was he? Dave couldn't figure out why everyone was laughing. He sat down on the old purple and green sofa, confused.

"Watch where you park your carcass!" yelped Grandad, as Dave sat on his elbow. "Serves me right for wearing my old green and purple shirt on this sofa. I was just catching a quick snooze, and the newspaper fell over my face."

"See what Dave's got for the Invisible Man," laughed Gran. "Look, it says 'guaranteed to float' right on the handle!"

Now Dave could explain the whole story about a ferry's wave swamping the little motor boat, and the flashlight sinking down, down, into the deep dark sea, until its glow disappeared ... *forever.*

And then he and Aunt Morna *had* to tell Rick every small detail, about catching their salmon. Aunt Morna hugged Dave, and called him a real salt water seaman, bringing the boat home safely even without a flashlight.

"He's a good man in a crisis," agreed Rick.

"That reminds me, Rick, we still have to stow the ladder under the verandah, and find my yellow hat. Then we're going over to Rick's place. We'll be back in lots of time to eat. OK if Rick comes back for dinner, Gran?"

Fifteen

They'd just finished the last of Monster's Marvellous Monsterburgers when they heard a shout that seemed to come from down on the bay. "I'm hearing voices again," laughed Dave. "This time they're real."

"Ahoy, there! Anybody home?" Louder, this time. Dave and Rick ran to the verandah, stopped in astonishment, and then ran straight on down the hill.

A small blue and white float plane was bobbing up and down at the end of the dock. Securing the mooring lines was a stranger, an extremely tall and skinny man, with a red cap and a fly-away grey beard. Who could it be?

"Sam's the name," bellowed the pilot. "Freelance reporter, from Salt Spring Island. Thought I'd do a story for the newspaper about the boy who found the scraper!"

"Actually, it was *both* of us," Dave called from half-way down the steps. "How did you know about the scraper? We only found it an hour ago!"

"Actually," replied the bearded man, "*You* told me, if you're Dave Jones. I'm Mr. Allen's grandson, Sam Stanley. We talked on the phone, remember? Hey, Dave, I've got some cargo here. Need your help. Must be more than a hundred steps," he declared, looking up the hill anxiously.

"Only ninety-nine, once you're on the shore," yelled Dave. "Sure, we'll help."

Just then, the 'cargo' came into plain sight. Stooping so that he wouldn't lose his blue baseball cap, a beaming Mr. Allen emerged through the plane's small doorway.

He waved at the boys with both arms and his grin stretched from ear to ear. He stopped smiling, though, when he noticed the ramp to the shore. It was steep and swaying and the hillside beyond was even steeper.

"No problem," called Dave, when he saw Mr. Allen's look of alarm. "This cargo isn't heavy. Rick and I can make a chair with our arms. We'll carry him up in style."

And so they did, stopping from time to time to discuss the 'log cabin that wasn't there', the giant cedar tree and the hole in it, the ladder, and Dave's battle scars.

Mr. Allen seemed to enjoy his ride. He was surprised when he saw how many trees still covered the hill. He declared that the newcomers hadn't ruined it, at least not completely.

Finally they reached the house, and Mr. Stanley and Aunt Morna took dozens of pictures, while Dave and Rick showed off the famous scraper. It was a noisy crowd.

Grandad lit the fire, and Mr. Allen sat in Gran's rocker close to the crackling logs. He held the little stone in the palm of his hand. Dave thought that his eyes looked misty. "It really is yours, isn't it?" he asked, watching Mr. Allen's face.

It's a good thing we found it this summer, thought Dave. *Next summer might have been too late. He really is old.* Dave felt a sudden chill, in spite of the warmth of the fire.

"It's quite amazing," Mr. Allen said, wiping the tears from his eyes. "I could hardly believe it when Sam told me about the phone call from Dave. This really is my scraper, folks. See, there's a little mark I put on it myself. But I'd know it, even without that."

"Now you've got it back, keep a good hold on it," said Dave. "Don't leave it in any more cedar trees."

"You're quite a boy Dave. First you solved the mystery about my game. Then you managed to hook up with Rick and you both found my lookout tree and my scraper! And all in a few days."

Mr. Allen turned to his grandson, Sam, and said shyly, "I wish you could write a book about this, not just a newspaper article."

"No time," said Mr. Stanley. "I've got another book to finish. How about Mr. or Mrs. Reid? I've heard you both write travel books."

They couldn't *possibly*. They were off to Australia again for a few months. Grandad suggested Aunt Morna.

"No way," she protested. "It should be someone who was part of the story."

"If you're looking at me, *forget* it," said Dave. "I have enough trouble writing letters!"

"Oh, no!" exploded Gran. "Dave, I'm sorry, I forgot to mail your letter. Stuff it in the pack, dear, along with your hypnotic sweater. Shade your eyes, because here it is, finished at last." She pulled it from behind her back and waved it like a flag.

Dave pounced on the letter and the wild sweater and added both to his pack. Yes, the sweater certainly was dazzling. His new friends in Chicago wouldn't mix *him* up with anyone else.

"Could I take *The Case of the Careless Carpet Beetle*?

And, ummm, could I borrow that big book about the Indians?"

Now his pack wouldn't quite close, but Dave had the solution. "I can take out the yellow hat," he decided, "the one that says 'Some Kid'. I'm saving it for Susie. Besides, if I wear it, it won't get squashed."

"Some kid, indeed," said Grandad, struggling to close the flap on the bulging pack. "Hope he's got a strong back."

"You know I could try writing that story," said Rick, who'd been sitting quietly beside Mr. Allen. "At least I could tell about finding the stone."

"*And* the puppy," added Dave. "Two discoveries in one...."

"I'm always scribbling stuff I make up," continued Rick, looking excited. "This one doesn't need making up. Should be a cinch. And part of it's about my own grandmother's uncle."

"What a great idea!" said Mr. Allen, rocking back and forth. "I'll be a living legend!"

"My goodness, look at the clock!" said Gran. "Just time for butter tarts."

"No thanks," said Rick, "not if they've got nuts in them. Raisins, yes. But not nuts, thank you. I'll pass them to, Mr. Allen, umm ... to THAA,WEN."

"I should have guessed about the butter tarts," laughed Gran. "Is it something to do with the name 'Jones'? These ones are raisins through and through. Eat fast. Mr. Stanley has to get his plane away before dark, and Morna and Dave absolutely *mustn't* miss the last ferry. His flight leaves tomorrow at the crack of dawn!"

Dave was still thinking about the story Rick would write. "Pardon me for being nosy," he said, giving Rick a poke in the ribs, "but what are you going to call this tale of adventure and discovery?"

"Seems to me that's up to Rick," protested Gran.

"He's writing it, and don't forget it's partly about his family history."

"No," said Rick, with a crooked smile. "The part about finding the scraper is actually because of Dave. If he hadn't been so crazy.... He was the one who had to climb that tree. Now it's part of this family's history too. You think of a name, Dave, something short and snappy."

"Secrets on the Shore," suggested Dave, but he wasn't really pleased about it. "Why don't we ask, Mr. Allen?"

"Who?" asked the old man, darting a piercing look at Dave. "Why don't you ask THAA,WEN? You still haven't called me by my Indian name."

"OK, then, ummm, THAA,WEN," said Dave. "What's a good title?"

"Well, it seems to me if Rick's writing about everything that happened today, it's all about Dinner Bay, and the voices that echoed across it. *You know*, the fog horns, and the puppy crying, and..."

"And when it comes to the cedar tree," added Dave, "it was your voice in my head, THAA,WEN, telling me I had to climb it."

"And then," continued Rick, "it was Dave shouting down, 'This is it, the perfect place!' and then 'Look out below!' "

"Then OUCH!" said Dave. He touched his bandaged head gingerly.

"And then," added Gran, "an unknown voice shouts 'Ahoy there, anybody home?'"

"And THAA,WEN makes his grand appearance!" chuckled Grandad. "Yes sir, this bay's seen and heard a lot today."

"So ..." said Dave, impatiently, "what's the title, *exactly*? Shouldn't it be something mysterious, sort of like a guessing game?" He stared at the old man in the rocking chair, expecting him to give the final word.

"I don't think you were listening," said THAA,WEN,

shaking his head sadly. "All the clues we've given you, they all point in the same direction."

"Eh? ... OK, OK, I've got it now," Dave shouted, flinging his arms and almost knocking the old man out of his chair. "How about Voices on the Bay? That'll keep them guessing, eh THAA,WEN!"

Acknowledgements

Thanks to the teachers, editors and friends who have guided and encouraged me. I am especially grateful to Earl Claxton Sr. and other teachers and students at the LAU,WELNEW Tribal School at Brentwood Bay, British Columbia, for sharing their personal knowledge of the Saanich People, past and present, and suggesting a real Indian name for one of my fictional characters. Thanks, as well, to Marie Elliott. Her comments and her book, *Mayne Island & Outer Gulf Islands, A History*, were extremely helpful.

My thanks to Anthony van Tulleken for allowing me to use his illustration of Reid's Roost.

Some of 'Gran's' family may *think* they recognize themselves, but in fact the truth has been stretched well into the realm of fiction. All other characters are completely fictitious.

The Author

Ginny, (Virginia Russell, neé Clippingdale) was born in Toronto, Ontario in 1931, grew up in Mississauga and taught primary grades there before the arrival of three daughters.

Vancouver has been her home since 1958, but she spent one year in Japan, and several shorter stays in Australia, England and the United States with her husband, a professor of Geophysics.

She credits a course given by Sue Ann Alderson in the Creative Writing Department at the University of British Columbia as a major step toward becoming an author.

Ginny's busy writing more stories at her new home in Ladner, B.C., or at her favourite 'escape' on Mayne Island.